"Maybe You Could Have Handled This Differently, *Figlio Mio*."

"You were the one who told me to marry her, Dad."

"Megan needed the Valente name. If you hadn't, I would have found a way to force you."

"Yeah, like you did with Alex and Nick."

"Naturally." There was a lengthy pause before Cesare spoke again. "What are you going to do now?"

"I'm not sure," Matt murmured, sounding distracted.

Lana, standing in the doorway, felt as though her breath had been cut off. They were talking about *her*.

And what was this about Alex and Nick? Cesare had forced them to marry their wives? He would have forced Nick to marry, too?

God, how many lives were the Valentes prepared to wreck for the sake of the family name?

Dear Reader,

This is the last book in my Valente series.
Matthew Valente may be the youngest of the three brothers, but he is no less compelling and commanding. And while he may be the last of the Valente men to get married, he unknowingly was the first to father a child.

Can you imagine finding out that you're the father of a little girl? Wouldn't the thought of having never found out upset you greatly? Your daughter could have grown up never knowing her father and you never knowing her. It's a heartbreaking thought.

Yet Lana Jensen has her reasons. And she's upset too. She knows she's in trouble when Matt discovers her secret. And did I mention that Matt is drop-dead handsome? ☺

I'm sad to say goodbye to my Valente men, but giving them all a happy ending with the women they love has been such a thrill for me. There's nothing better than being a writer.

Happy reading!

Maxine

VALENTE'S BABY

MAXINE SULLIVAN

Published by Silhouette Books
America's Publisher of Contemporary Romance

SILHOUETTE BOOKS

ISBN-13: 978-0-373-76949-0

VALENTE'S BABY

Copyright © 2009 by Maxine Sullivan

Recycling programs
for this product may
not exist in your area.

This edition published by arrangement with Harlequin Books S.A.

® and TM are trademarks of Harlequin Books S.A., used under license. Trademarks indicated with ® are registered in the United States Patent and Trademark Office, the Canadian Trade Marks Office and in other countries.

Visit Silhouette Books at www.eHarlequin.com

Printed in U.S.A.

Books by Maxine Sullivan

Silhouette Desire

*The Millionaire's Seductive Revenge #1782
*The Tycoon's Blackmailed Mistress #1800
*The Executive's Vengeful Seduction #1818
Mistress & a Million Dollars #1855
The CEO Takes a Wife #1883
The C.O.O. Must Marry #1926
Valente's Baby #1949

*Australian Millionaires

MAXINE SULLIVAN

credits her mother for her lifelong love of romance novels, so it was a natural extension for Maxine to want to write her own romances. She thinks there's nothing better than being a writer and is thrilled to be one of the few Australians to write for the Silhouette Desire line.

Maxine lives in Melbourne, Australia, but over the years has traveled to New Zealand, the UK and the U.S.A. In her own backyard, her husband's job ensured they saw the diversity of the countryside, from the tropics to the outback, country towns to the cities. She is married to Geoff, who has proven his hero status many times over the years. They have two handsome sons and an assortment of much-loved, previously abandoned animals.

Maxine would love to hear from you and can be contacted through her Web site at www.maxinesullivan.com.

To the three men in my life—
my husband, Geoff, and sons, Anthony and Kevin.
You are my heart.

One

"You're a father."

Matt Valente broke into a grin as he sat down on the hotel bed. "I didn't know I was pregnant."

"Don't be smart, Matthew," Cesare Valente snapped down the telephone line. The founder of the House of Valente perfume dynasty was clearly not amused. "Remember Lana Jensen?"

The smile dropped from Matt's lips. "She was my top accountant a while back, so yeah, I should remember her." That perfect body…that beautiful face…those Nordic blue eyes hinting at a Scandinavian heritage that seemed as clear as crystal but were in fact deep and hiding lies.

"She had your baby."

A baby?

No way.

The only thing she'd *had* was him.

They'd both been a little tipsy at the office Christmas party and she'd taken advantage of his inebriated state to seduce him. They'd made love on the sofa in his office.

Not that he'd been any less to blame for succumbing to her charms, despite her giving him the come-on for months, her blue gaze skittering away every so often, teasing him with a sensual game of cat and mouse.

Afterward he'd regretted not keeping to his golden rule of no personal involvement with office staff. As chief financial officer for the family business, he didn't need any complications in the workplace.

"I don't believe it. She's lying."

"I saw the child with my own eyes, Matt. I was in my Mercedes waiting for the light to change when Lana crossed in front of me pushing a small child in a stroller. I checked out the birth certificate. Your name's on it."

Matt's hand tightened around the phone. "Dad, that's a breach of privacy."

His.

Hell, if *his* name was on that birth certificate he needed to sort it out.

"Matt, I did what needed to be done. And that included a background check on Lana."

Matt's lips twisted. "Why am I not surprised?"

"It was necessary. She's the mother of my grandchild."

"And she'd suitable?" he asked with a touch of sarcasm.

"As far as I'm concerned, yes. Her parents are dead, and she has an uncle who lives in France and is a respected businessman. Do you want to know more? There's some other information on her family. I can send you the report."

"No, thanks." He knew all he needed to know about Lana Jensen. More than enough.

And he needed to make his father see sense.

"Dad, look, you can put any name on a birth certificate. I didn't think you'd fall for that old trick."

"She's a Valente, *figlio mio.*" *Son of mine.* "She looked just like you. There's no doubt in my mind."

Something odd bounced around in Matt's chest. "It's a girl? Er…I mean, she's a girl?"

"Yes. And I'm delighted. It's about time we had another little girl in the family."

Matt grimaced. Girl or boy, it didn't matter to him. "Well, I'm not."

"You will be once you see her."

"Who said I was going to see her?"

"She's my granddaughter, Matt. If you don't go to her, then I'll bring her to you."

Matt's jaw clenched. "This is to trick me into getting married, isn't it? You may have forced Alex and Nick to marry, but I'm not falling for it, Dad."

A year ago they'd been about to branch into the North American market with their top-selling perfume, Valente's Woman, when Cesare had threatened to sell the business out from under Alex's feet if he didn't marry. Then a couple of months ago, Cesare had promised to give the Valente estate to anyone but his second son, Nick. Both his brothers had been given no choice but to do what their father wanted or lose what they loved most. As youngest son, Matt had decided there was nothing his father could do to him to make him marry.

"Matt, I admit I had no compunction in forcing your two brothers to marry, and I would have found a way to force you to marry, too. Only now I don't have to, do I? You've brought a daughter into this world and you will give that daughter your name. She will be known as a true Valente."

"Don't dictate to me, Dad. If this child is mine, and I'm in no way convinced of it, then I'll give her my name. You can count on it."

"That's all I wanted to know. The family jet is at Brisbane Airport waiting for you. Nick and Sasha are already there and will attend the conference dinner in your place."

His father was like a damn bulldozer at times. Not even the heart attack had stopped his interfering in his sons' lives.

"I've got a date for the dinner tonight."

"You *had* a date. I suggest you break it and get back to Sydney tonight and go see the mother of

your child as soon as possible. I like Lana and I'm
sure she'll be reasonable."

At the mention of Lana, his gut clenched, but
there was no way he wanted his father to know that.
Cesare would somehow use that knowledge in
future if he could. He could imagine the older man's
reaction if he ever told him Lana was a thief and that
he'd covered up for her without telling anyone. And
he couldn't wholly blame his decision not to report
their theft on Cesare's heart attack at the time either.

"What woman is ever reasonable, Dad?" he
mocked.

Cesare laughed and said goodbye, and Matt hung
up the phone and went to stand at the window in his
hotel suite. He looked out over the sweeping coast-
line of Queensland's Gold Coast as the rolling surf
of the Pacific Ocean tumbled onto the golden beaches
of Australia's tourist capital.

Tonight he'd planned a romantic dinner and a
night of lovemaking with a lady friend of his.

Now he could only think of one woman.

Lana Jensen.

She'd been the only woman he'd made love to
without a condom. He'd been so hot for her, and the
alcohol he'd consumed had lowered his guard.

But if that child was his—if Lana had lied to
him about being protected from a pregnancy—then
she'd done more than stolen that fifty thousand
dollars from the House of Valente.

She'd just stolen his freedom.

* * *

"Oh my God!" Lana gasped a split second after opening her apartment door and seeing the man on the other side. Panic raced through her at the speed of light. It couldn't be him. It just couldn't be.

"Yes, you'd better start praying," Matt Valente declared.

Recovering hastily, she played for time even as she edged the door shut a fraction. "Matt, what are you doing here?"

"You know the answer to that."

"I do?"

"Invite me in, Lana."

Not for all the tea in China.

"Sorry, no. I'm going out shortly." She started shutting the door with more haste. "Perhaps if you have something to say you can telephone me tomorrow and—"

He pushed past her into the apartment, despite his haste, gently moving her out of the way. "I've got plenty to say and I intend on saying it *now.*"

She tried to hold back her agitation. "Look, you just can't come in here and—"

"Where is she, Lana?"

Lana froze. "Where is who?"

"My daughter."

Dear Lord, until that moment she'd been hoping this wasn't what his visit was about.

"So you know?" she whispered.

"It's true, then."

She bit her lip. "No. I mean…er…sure, I had a baby but—"

"Give it up, Lana. She's my daughter. My father saw you with her on the street and he checked out her birth certificate."

She gaped at him. "But…but that's an invasion of my privacy."

"Do you think he cares?"

Just then a child's babble issued from the living room and Matt shot her a dark look.

Lana stepped in front of him. "Matt, please. Just leave. Don't do this."

"No chance in hell," he growled, and stepped around her, taking a few paces to the doorway. He went stone still as he saw the little toddler standing up against the playpen railings.

Lana tried not to think about how he must be feeling right now. She told herself not to feel sorry for him. Matt Valente was a playboy who wasn't ready to settle down or have children. If he was here, it was only because his father had made him come.

"What's her name?"

Surprise kicked in. "You don't know?"

He didn't move a muscle. "What's her name?" he said rawly.

"Megan."

A moment slid by, then, "Megan Valente."

Apprehension slithered down Lana's spine. "Actually, it's Megan Jensen."

"Soon it will be Valente," he said with the full superiority of a Valente male.

Her mind reeled. "What do you mean?"

He ignored the question as he walked over to Megan, crouched down in front of the eleven-month-old and looked at her through the bars.

Lana could see his reflection in the decorative wall mirror. There was awesome wonder on his handsome face as he took in each and every feature of the beautiful little girl.

Her heart tilted. For Megan's sake she wanted Matt to love his daughter. For her own sake she wanted him to deny parentage, leave and never come back.

"Hello, Megan," Matt said softly, not touching, not moving, not doing anything except capturing her attention.

Megan stared back entranced, her brown eyes so like her father's. She looked so cute, a little dark-haired doll with chubby cheeks and bow-shaped lips that had recently learned to blow a sloppy kiss for her mother.

Oh God.

Suddenly Megan transferred her gaze to Lana and within the space of a second her face began to screw up and she let out a wail.

Lana rushed forward and lifted her out of the playpen. "It's her bedtime," she said, soothing her daughter with a "shh" and patting her back until the little girl hiccupped and quieted.

Matt got to his feet, his expression unreadable. "Put her to bed, then we'll talk."

She hesitated.

"Put her to bed, Lana."

"If you insist." She hitched Megan higher on her hip. "Take a seat. I'll be back in a minute."

"No. I'm coming with you."

She swallowed. That sounded ominous. "Why?"

"I'm interested in everything my daughter does."

"*Our* daughter."

"At least you're admitting it now."

Trying not to show how upset she was with all this, she hurried past him and down the hallway to the smaller bedroom. She had stenciled Megan's room with a variety of farm animals, adding a musical mobile that played a lullaby above the crib, and giving her daughter plenty of soft toys to cuddle. The room looked lovely.

Megan had fully settled down by now as Lana changed her diaper. She lay there quietly, her eyes on Matt in the doorway as if she was fascinated by him despite herself.

Don't let him get to you, sweetheart, Lana wanted to say. *Ignore him and he'll go away.*

She hoped.

Then she kissed Megan on the cheek. "Good night, pumpkin," she murmured, then put her in her crib.

She was grateful when Matt stepped back to allow her to leave the now-darkened room without having to squeeze past him. "Coffee?" she said, heading for the kitchen, needing something to do.

"Don't you have something stronger?"

She shot him a look over her shoulder. "Sorry. I don't usually drink."

"Yeah, I remember."

His sarcasm had her spinning to face him. "That was different. It was Christmas and—"

"You thought I'd be a good lay."

The breath caught in her throat. "It wasn't like that."

"It wasn't? Then perhaps you thought I'd be a good sperm donor and future moneymaker?"

"No! I—"

She'd been so attracted to Matt back then, and working for him the two years previously had made her crazy with want. Yet in spite of them both having a few drinks too many, it hadn't been cheap.

Not for her anyway.

It had been intense and overwhelming, and she hadn't been able to help herself when she'd literally run into him coming out of the elevator as she went to collect her purse from her desk after the party. He'd held her to stop her from falling and that had been all it needed. She'd lifted her mouth up toward his and he'd groaned and backed her into his office.

"Yes?" he prompted now, a sudden sensual look in his eyes telling her he remembered.

Everything.

"Let's just forget it," she muttered. "We both acted out of character that night."

"Oh, I'd say you acted right *in* character. You knew exactly what you were doing."

She swiveled away before he could see the hurt in her eyes. If he knew her he'd realize she'd never seduce a man just to father a child. Forcing a man to be a father never worked.

With shaking hands she put the coffeepot on, then took a ragged breath and turned to face the one person who could unravel her perfectly constructed life once again.

He stood with his lower back against the sink, his arms crossed against a well-muscled chest.. "So, Lana, you lied to me, didn't you? You told me afterward that you were on contraceptives. You told me there was nothing to worry about." His eyes seared her. "But there was, wasn't there?"

She hesitated, then, "Yes."

"Did you think I would tell you to get rid of it?"

She hesitated again, but only briefly. "The thought did cross my mind."

"No bloody way!"

An odd feeling turned inside her chest at his emphatic reply. She'd thought about that scenario of course, but had come to the conclusion Matt would want his child. Playboy or not, he had strong family ethics, and if he'd known he was about to be a father, nothing would have stopped him from being involved in the baby's life.

And now he knew.

God help her.

"You should have told me as soon as you realized you were pregnant."

Her throat turned dry. "I couldn't, Matt."

"Why?"

She hadn't wanted to risk him taking her child away from her. If he'd thought his son or daughter was better off with the Valentes, he would have had no hesitation in instigating a custody battle.

And he'd have won, too.

She'd seen it time and again at the boarding school her uncle Dan had paid for her to attend. Some of the rich thought they were above reproach. That money and privilege gave them the right to do what they liked. Usually, they got their way.

He could still win.

She swallowed hard. She couldn't tell him the truth. If he knew her fears…if he knew she'd do anything to keep her daughter…he'd take advantage of her biggest vulnerability.

Her love for her child.

"I realized you wouldn't want to be a father." That was true. "You're far too busy being a playboy. The two things don't mix."

"I'm a father now, and you don't see me running."

"We both know you feel obligated and nothing more."

"Don't presume to know what I'm feeling." A pulse

beat in his cheekbone. "Why put my name on the birth certificate if you didn't want the truth known?"

That had been her one weakness.

"I had to," she admitted. "In case anything ever happened to me. I needed her to know."

He gave her a look sharper than a knife. "Were you ever going to tell me, Lana? And what about our daughter? When were you going to tell her?"

She inclined her head. "When she was older. It would have been up to her to decide whether she wanted to make contact with you."

"And in the meantime you would have poisoned her against me. And I would have missed out on her growing up." His eyes stabbed her with his disgust. "So you're a cheat and a liar as well as a thief?"

"No, I…" She shook her head to clear it. "*What* did you say?"

Then she got it.

"Matt, I know you may think my keeping Megan from you is stealing but—"

"I meant the money you stole from the House of Valente."

Her fine brows drew together. "Money?"

"Don't play dumb, lady. Remember that little sum of fifty thousand dollars? I found the paperwork after you left. You covered your tracks well, but not well enough to fool me."

She rocked back in shock. "I didn't steal any money."

"You're lying again."

She shook her head. "No, I'm not."

"Don't play games. You're caught out. There's nothing you can say to convince me otherwise."

A threat of hysteria rose in her throat. "I didn't steal any money. I wouldn't. I'm an accountant, for heaven's sake. I'd lose my job and my livelihood."

"Which is part of why I didn't report the theft. For some reason I felt I owed you that. Lord knows why," he said with total self-possession. "If my father hadn't had his heart attack, I might have changed my mind."

"You should have reported it. At least then I could have proven you wrong."

"That's not possible."

"Look, if you think I stole money, what did I do with it, then?"

He glanced around the kitchen, with its shiny new appliances. "The deposit for this apartment must have been expensive."

She blinked in surprise. He didn't know that her uncle Dan had bought this apartment for her? How could he not know? She was sure he would have checked out her background and found out all sorts of things about her family.

Or perhaps that was still in the works.

If it was, then no doubt Matt would discover how wrong he was about this stolen money.

If it wasn't, no way would she tell him anything. Her uncle Dan had been very kind to her and she loved him dearly, and she wouldn't repay him by having the Valentes delve into his private life. She knew that her uncle was bisexual, with him married to Aimee but having a gay lover, Julien. It wasn't common knowledge, and she'd only found out about Julien on their last visit to Australia—the same time Dan had discovered she was pregnant.

She couldn't—wouldn't—open Dan's personal life up for gossip. Not even to prove to Matt that she wasn't the person he thought she was.

"What? No answer?" he mocked.

She lifted her chin. "You're wrong about me."

"I don't think so." His eyes hardened further. "Now it's payback time."

"Payback?" The fine hairs on her arms rose in warning.

"We're getting married. For a year, so that my daughter will be known as a Valente."

Her mind stumbled in shock. She'd never expected him to offer marriage. She didn't come from a moneyed background, nor was she of good stock. Marriage to Matt Valente just hadn't been an option.

And she wouldn't have pushed for that option even if it *had* been. She'd sworn never to marry for the sake of a child. She wouldn't make the same mistake her mother had made, she'd promised herself years ago. Megan would not grow up in a hostile household like Lana had. There was nothing as bad as a husband who felt trapped. It brought out the worst in a man.

She shuddered. Her own mother had been pregnant with *her* when she'd married Lana's father. Valerie Jensen had loved her husband and she'd prayed he would come to love her in return, only he hadn't. He'd used that love against her every day of their married live.

Would Matt do the same?

Somehow Lana managed a strangled, "This is ludicrous. You can acknowledge Megan as your daughter without marrying *me*."

"No. I want this official. I already have the license for this Friday at three o'clock." She gasped but he ignored it. "Believe me, Lana, if you try to run I'll find you and I'll make sure the judge at the custody hearing learns all about how you stole money, about how you always put yourself first, how you were unwilling to give your daughter the best in life, and how you put Megan's life at risk by running. I'll get full custody of *my* daughter. And that's not a threat, that's a promise."

"You wouldn't," she muttered. It was her worst nightmare.

The line of his mouth flattened. "Try me."

"She's my daughter, Matt. I carried her and I gave birth to her while you were out sleeping around with other women. You have very little right to her."

A nerve pulsed near his temple. "I'm her father. But don't worry. I don't plan on sleeping with you. We'll have separate bedrooms."

"For all your comings and goings?" She shook her head. "I won't have you parading your girl-friends in front of Megan."

"I'll take no lovers for the next year. And that's out of respect for my child, not you."

Defeat weighed heavily on her shoulders, but she was determined not to let him see it. She tried to think and could only come up with one thing that might help her.

"Okay, but I'll only marry you if I can come back to work for you. I want to find the real thief." She would prove her innocence without bringing Dan into it.

"Do you really think that's going to happen?" he scoffed.

"I mean it, Matt," she said, remaining firm but knowing she didn't have a leg to stand on if he refused her request.

He shrugged. "As you wish. But just don't plan on stealing any more money from us."

His comment offended her. "If I wanted to do that I'd steal it from my current job, wouldn't I?"

He looked surprised. "You work?"

The question would have amused her at any other time. "I have to earn a living somehow."

"Not anymore," he dismissed arrogantly. "I'll support you and Megan. There's no need for you to work at all."

He was unbelievable!

"I *like* working. It's part of who I am." She saw his eyes narrow and realized she was giving away too much about herself. She didn't want that.

Nor did she want to be supported by him, she

decided, getting back to the point. It would only be for Megan's sake if she accepted a little help from him.

And come to think of it, this would actually work out well. The one thing she regretted as a single mum was not having as much time to spend with her daughter as she'd like.

"I'll work a couple days with you and the other days I plan on staying home with Megan. Agreed?"

He paused, then, "Agreed."

"But after the year's up, I get my divorce, right?" She couldn't imagine being connected to this Valente for longer than that. "Promise me, Matt."

"I can guarantee it."

Two

"If any person can show just cause why these two people may not be joined together, let him speak now or forever hold their peace."

Lana's heart fluttered with anxiety in the ensuing silence, wishing that someone…anyone…would put a stop to this lunacy. If only Megan would cry, she might have the confidence to say no to this marriage.

The registrar continued with the ceremony.

And suddenly it was too late.

"You may now kiss each other."

Oh Lord.

As if Matt knew that she couldn't look at him to save her life right now, he put his hand on her arm and turned her toward him, a solemn look in his eyes.

He lowered his head and she repressed a shiver; in the mere few days since he'd come back into her life she could not ignore his compelling presence.

And then his lips touched hers in a precise kiss that said he was cool and in control and in no way did he want a response from her.

She was glad to oblige.

It would be her secret that his touch still made her tingle. She'd take that secret to the grave, she knew, as he moved back, his eyes dark and inscrutable.

The registrar smiled at the small gathering. "I present to you Mr. and Mrs. Matthew Valente."

Her heart dipped, but Matt's family—their only guests—started congratulating them, giving Lana time to compose herself. She'd told them she had no family to invite, except an aunt and uncle who were off on a jaunt to South Africa. Of course, it was the truth, but she played it low-key. And she hadn't wanted to invite the few single friends she'd drifted away from since having Megan.

The Valentes were it.

Yet she couldn't complain about their treatment of her. They were just so delighted to have a new addition in Megan, and they even seemed genuinely pleased *she* was joining them. She'd thought they might think she'd tried to trap Matt, but Cesare and Isabel had been kindness itself.

She could even set aside her resentment with Cesare for his breach of privacy over the birth certificate, after he'd handed her a gorgeous posy of flowers on arrival today, the bright colors a perfect foil against the soft femininity of her cream suit.

And Isabel had put one of the flowers from the posy in Megan's dark hair. Both gestures had been a little "family" touch that had overwhelmed Lana and she'd had to blink rapidly to hold back the tears.

"We need a photograph of the bride and groom, and then one of the whole family," Isabel said, pulling Lana from her thoughts.

"Smile," Matt murmured, smiling at her. "I want my family to at least think we can be pleasant to each other."

"That'll be a stretch."

He blinked at her words, and gave a low chuckle, and she found herself smiling back genuinely for the first time.

At that moment the camera clicked.

"Hey, that'll be a great picture," Nick said, looking at the screen on the digital camera. "Yes, it is. Now let's try a few more, and then we'll get someone to take a picture of us all together."

Lana continued to smile, but she was grateful the camera hadn't clicked a moment ago, or it might have caught her expression reeling from the effects of Matt's devastating smile.

Matt Valente could only be described as terminally handsome, with his sophisticated good looks and attitude of self-command making a woman hard-pressed to turn her eyes away.

And he was now her husband.

And Megan's father, she reminded herself, not allowing herself to forget the reason she was here today.

After the photographs, everyone headed out of the building to go to Cesare and Isabel's apartment, where a late lunch with the family was to be held in their honor.

Lana had just climbed into the limousine when there was a flash as someone raced up and snapped a picture of them. Thankfully she'd been blocking a view of Megan at the time.

Matt swore and quickly shut the door behind them. "Bloody journalists," he growled. "I don't like them taking pictures of Megan."

Lana's brow rose in surprise. She felt the same but, "Isn't the point of our marriage to get her known as a Valente?"

"Not with pictures. I was raised in front of the press, but it's a different world now and I'll be damned if I'll let them use her. That's not what our marriage is about."

His words warmed her and she quickly buried her face in her daughter's dark curls. For the first time she didn't feel as though Megan would be alone in the world if anything happened to *her*. Dan would do his best from France of course, but it wasn't the same as being cared for by a father who loved her.

She'd marry a thousand men like Matt to do this for her daughter, she admitted, then realized how ridiculous that thought was. There *was* no other man like Matt Valente.

Alex and Nick Valente were men in their own right.

And so was Matt.

He was one of a kind.

And he knew it.

Lana couldn't help but feel a little reserved once they arrived at his parents' apartment. Matt stayed by her side for a while, then left her to walk around with Megan in his arms.

As she watched him she wished she could believe that their daughter was some sort of trophy to him, but she knew that wasn't true. He was a proud father, that's all.

Occasionally he'd look her way and he'd smile at her for the benefit of the others, but Lana was sure they weren't fooling any of them. She only had to look at his two brothers to see the truth in their eyes. They knew Megan was the reason Matt had married her.

As did their wives, Olivia and Sasha. Olivia was the daughter of a famous movie star, which had to be hard at times. And poor Sasha's father had been charged with fraud and was due to be sentenced soon.

Yet both women were just so nice and unaffected by the trappings of wealth. They even mentioned getting together for lunch, but Lana held them off.

And she planned on holding them off for as long as she could. It was no use her getting too close to these women. She'd be gone before they knew it, she told herself, sipping at her champagne and watching Alex and Olivia's eight-year-old son, Scott, and their newly adopted six-year-old daughter, Renee, playing together.

Just then Matt moved into her line of vision to talk to Alex. Megan was still in his arms and her poor darling was cautiously looking up at her father as if she wasn't sure whether to cry or not.

And Matt wasn't letting go.

And didn't she know how *that* felt? Matt was paying no notice to Megan's nervousness, just as he paid no notice to *hers*.

Suddenly Matt looked at Megan and kissed her cheek and without warning Megan gave her toothless little grin. Lana's heart tripped over when she saw that.

Megan and Matt would be okay together.

"You've done the right thing for her," Isabel said gently, coming up beside Lana.

Lana started, then gave a small smile. "I know, Isabel."

"Matt will be good for her."

"Yes, he will." She would never have married him if he wasn't.

"And you'll be good for my son."

Lana wrinkled her nose. "I'm not so sure about that."

"*I* am. He needs someone like you."

Lana shook her head. "No, you're wrong. I'm nothing special." Matt needed someone who liked to go out and party. And probably someone from a high-profile family would be even better.

The older woman considered her. "Don't put yourself down, Lana. You're a lovely person, and any woman who puts her child first like you're doing by marrying my son is someone we're proud to have in our family."

Lana swallowed hard and blinked rapidly, touched by the words. "Most mothers would do what I'm doing."

"No, sweetie, they wouldn't," Isabel said, turning to gaze at her three sons.

Lana remembered then that Isabel was actually Alex and Nick's stepmother, not their real mother as she was Matt's. From what she knew of the Valentes, Alex's mother had died when he was little and Cesare had then married Nick's mother, who'd walked out when Nick was a baby. Cesare had then found long-term happiness with his third wife, Isabel, who'd been a proper mother to the three boys.

Lana inclined her head. "You're right, Isabel. Not all mothers are the same."

A short time later, Cesare tapped his champagne glass with a spoon to get everyone's attention.

"First of all, I'd like to congratulate my youngest son and his new wife on their marriage." He held up his glass. "To Lana and Matt. May your marriage be strong and happy."

"To Lana and Matt," the others toasted, and Lana

felt her cheeks warm. Was she the only one to see that cynical look in Matt's eyes?

"And now," Cesare said, "Izzie and I have a special gift for all our beautiful daughters-in-law. To each of you, we give the very first of our new Valente's Woman Limited Edition perfume."

Isabel handed out the gorgeous bottles of scent and Lana was grateful Olivia and Sasha's excitement made her own more sedate response fade into the background. She felt like such a fraud. She didn't deserve to be a part of this. She only had to look at Matt to know he was thinking the same thing.

Thankfully, the party finally ended two hours later. Megan was tired and had begun to cry and Matt declared they were leaving, for which Lana was relieved. It had been a long afternoon and Megan had been a little angel through it all, but now she needed her bed.

And that bed should now be at Matt's place. In the days leading up to the wedding she hadn't thought to ask where that was, but he'd told her he'd have all Megan's things and anything Lana wanted transferred to his apartment while they were busy with the ceremony.

Twenty minutes later Matt turned the car into the gated driveway of a large house that had a picturesque garden and lawn. Then she saw the high fence had a board with a Sold sign across it.

She twisted toward Matt in disbelief. "Tell me you didn't buy this house for us?"

His satisfied look completely disappeared. "Yes, I did."

"When?"

"Yesterday."

Her eyes widened. "But we're only going to be married for a year."

"So? It'll be a good investment. Anyway, my apartment wasn't suitable for a child."

"I can just imagine," she muttered.

His eyes turned cold. "There were only two bedrooms."

"I could have shared with Megan."

She certainly wouldn't have shared with *him*.

"Megan needs her own space." He paused. "And you need your sleep if you insist on working."

Okay, so she couldn't fault that.

Her irritation subsided a little; then she thought of something else. "You could have just left us at my apartment, you know. And you could've stayed at yours."

"No."

Her lips pressed together, even though she hadn't much hope he'd agree. "I've lived there for almost a year now. There's nothing wrong with it."

"That doesn't mean it's suitable for Megan."

That stung.

"I see." Obviously *she* could live in a dump for all he cared, but Megan needed to live somewhere befitting the Valente name.

Then she felt bad.

It sounded as though she was jealous of her daughter, and she wasn't. *She* had the Valente name herself now anyway, even if she wasn't going to use it, having decided to stick to Jensen. After hearing herself referred to as Mrs. Matthew Valente at the Registry Office today, she needed this to keep a sense of independence.

No, it was Matt's dominating way that really irked her. He thought he knew what was best for her and Megan. He should have asked her opinion.

Clearly having had enough, Matt pushed open his car door. "Come on. Let's go inside." He got out of the car and opened the back door, ducking back in to release Megan from her car seat. "Leave her things. I'll get them later."

Lana alighted and then went to take Megan out of his arms. "Here. Give her to me."

"No, she's heavy. I'll carry her." He walked away and up the front steps, leaving Lana to grit her teeth and follow them.

Matt produced a key and opened the door wide and they stepped into an entry foyer. A glimpse at the formal living room on the right confirmed the place was stunning.

"Did you even take the time to look around before you bought this place? You didn't, did you?"

His aristocratic brow rose. "Why? It's not good enough?"

She waved a dismissive hand, parroting his offhandedness. "Don't be crazy. It's lovely. I just wondered, that's all."

"I always think before I act, Lana."

Not always, was her immediate thought as their eyes met and she saw that same thought in him. She flushed. The one time he *hadn't* thought things through was the reason they were here now.

"We have a housekeeper starting tomorrow," he said, somewhat in a clipped tone. "She has her own apartment at the back of the house."

She nodded and glanced down the hallway as if she was looking around, but it was more about not looking at *him*.

"I'll give you a tour later. For now I'll show you the bedrooms." He started down the hallway and she tensed as once again she followed him until he turned left into a wing. He opened the first door. "This is your room. You've got your own en suite."

At least they didn't have to share a bathroom. Nor that beautiful, king-size bed, which she pretended she didn't even notice. "Very nice."

"There's a connecting door to Megan's room." He walked to the next room. "This is hers." He pointed to the door farther along. "My room's next to this one."

Lana's heart missed a beat as the impact of their circumstances started to roll over her. She was going to be sharing a house with the man who had the monopoly on high-powered virility.

God help her.

All of a sudden Megan saw her crib and squirmed to get to it. "She wants to go to bed."

Matt nodded. "Everything's here, so I'll leave you to it while I go get the rest of her things from the car."

"Okay. Just put her down on the carpet while I get organized."

Once he'd left, Lana stood looking around. Megan's furniture appeared miniscule in this room that was painted in pale yellow with nursery rhyme characters stenciled around the walls. Her daughter was going to love looking at them from her crib.

But for now…

"Right, madam. Let me get out of this jacket first," Lana said, slipping off her cream jacket and placing it on a chair, leaving her cream camisole top above her short skirt. "That's better."

She gathered a few items. "Now it's your turn."

Lifting Megan up, she laid her on the change table while she gave her a top-and-tail with a wash-cloth and then put on a clean diaper.

She chatted as she went. "You were such a good little girl today. Mummy is very proud of you. I think you…"

Five minutes later Matt stood in the doorway, letting Lana's voice flow over him as he watched her preparing Megan for bed. It was an odd feeling watching these two new women in his life.

His daughter he loved already.

And the other he….wanted.

His gaze traveled over Lana's profile. Her short blond hair was always stylish, but she'd done something special to it today and it looked fantastic.

Her cream suit fit her perfectly, but now she'd taken off her jacket and was standing there in a lacy top with spaghetti straps curved over her shoulders, leaving her smooth skin free.

And that short skirt and silk stockings showcased her long legs, one of which she'd kicked out behind her as she leaned over their daughter on the change table.

His groan kicked into gear in reply. This woman had to be the sexiest mother he'd ever seen.

And dammit, he still desired her.

As if sensing his presence, she looked over at him and he quickly blanked out his expression. It was going to be tough enough being in the same house, without her knowing that he wanted to strip those clothes from her body.

"You'll have to teach me how to do that," he said, determined not to let her know his thoughts.

Her elegant eyebrows rose a fraction. "*You'll* change her diaper?"

"I think I should know how to do these things. I want to be a hands-on father."

She relaxed with a wry smile. "Oh, changing diapers will certainly give you that experience," she said, picking Megan up in her arms and turning toward the crib, but not before Lana's smile swept into him.

"Wait," he managed to say as he approached them. "I want to give her a good-night kiss." He leaned forward to kiss his daughter's chubby cheek. "Sweet dreams, Megan Valente." She smelled of baby powder.

But as he eased back he caught a tantalizing hint of "Valente's Woman," the special perfume that was taking the world by storm. All the Valente women wore it—and now Lana was truly entitled to wear it, too.

It suited her.

Only for a year, he reminded himself, growing angry with disappointment at the woman she was. Damn her for stealing that money. He didn't want a thief for a wife, or for the mother of his child.

A year, that's all.

And then she could damn well wear whatever perfume she pleased.

"There's some food and coffee in the kitchen," he snapped, as he walked to the door.

"Thank you, but I'll be fine."

He stopped to look at her. "Neither of us had much to eat today."

"You'll join me?" she said with clear surprise.

"Is that a problem?"

She sent him a cautious glance. "No, I guess not."

"The kitchen's down the hallway on the right," he said, leaving them alone.

He hated that her attraction got to him. She was

fiery and icy at the same time, and watching her just now only served to remind him what he could have if he chose to bed her.

He cursed under his breath. This wasn't the way it was supposed to be. And definitely not from their first day together.

Five minutes later she entered the kitchen. She'd slipped her jacket back on, but if she thought it would provide some sort of protective shield she was very much mistaken. The fine material might have veiled the bare shoulders and firm breasts beneath her camisole top, but the clingy fabric couldn't fully conceal the outline of that willowy figure beneath her short skirt.

She caught him looking at her and her blue eyes flared before darting away to nervously glance around the room.

Look at me again, he wanted to say, then immediately severed the thought.

Don't look.

Don't touch.

"This is a magnificent kitchen, Matt," she began to chatter, still looking everywhere but at him. "Your housekeeper is sure to love it."

"She's your housekeeper, too," he pointed out.

Her gaze flew to him. "But I've never had a housekeeper before."

"You're a Valente now. You'll have to get used to it."

Anger flashed in her eyes; then her chin angled.

"Actually, I'm keeping my own name. Megan's the Valente now, not me."

The comment shouldn't have surprised him, but it did. Most women he knew would jump at any chance to be Mrs. Valente.

He frowned. Or was her show of independence merely for his benefit? She might not have wanted this marriage, but she certainly knew how to take advantage of an opportunity.

"So you're a liberated woman?" he drawled, not bothering to make an issue of it. He had her measure.

"I don't see any point in taking on a name I have no intention of keeping."

He gave a careless shrug. "Fair enough."

She stared for a moment. "You're not going to argue about it?"

"No. I agree. It makes sense."

"Oh." She seemed to be at a loss. "Good." Then she swung away and viewed the selection of food on the marble countertop. "This all looks very appetizing."

The muscles at the back of his neck were taut. The only thing that looked appetizing was *her*. "My mother thought we might be hungry."

"That's sweet of her."

Funny, his mother had called Lana sweet. It worried him. He didn't want his family drawn in or upset by her. His parents would be shocked if they knew what she was really like. It would be a hard pill to swallow knowing that the mother of their grandchild was so untrustworthy.

He gestured for her to sit on one of the tall stools. "Help yourself to the food," he said tightly, moving around the other side of the countertop, not wanting to be too close to her right now.

She slid onto the stool and picked up one of the delicious-looking sandwiches, appearing to be at ease, but he knew she was anything but.

He took one of the sandwiches for himself. "Speaking of my mother, you were having a good chat with her this evening," he said casually, remembering how he'd watched them and felt the urgent need to part the two women.

A wary look crossed her face, then vanished. "Were we?"

"You both looked deep in conversation."

"Then we probably were," she said, and took a nibble of her sandwich.

His brows drew together. It appeared as though she was hiding behind that sandwich, not eating it. That made him suspicious.

"I hope you're not planning on worming your way into her good books."

Her eyes widened and the sandwich lowered from her mouth. "Why would I do that?"

"My mother is predisposed to liking you. That makes her vulnerable to being hurt."

She frowned. "I don't plan on hurting her. Or anyone else for that matter."

"Don't you?"

She slowly put the sandwich down on the plate

and shot him a glare. "You know, you really are a bastard."

All at once everything within him rose like bile. "No, my daughter was the bastard."

She drew in a sharp breath. "I can't believe you just said that."

"You don't like to hear the truth?" The air held tight with tension. "I'm suddenly married to a treacherous beauty who not only stole money from my family, but who stole almost a year of my daughter's life from me. I think I have fifty thousand and one reasons to be pretty damn angry right now, don't you?"

Her chin angled. "You may think that, and that's your choice, but you've also got one very good reason for at least showing me some respect as your wife. And *she's* in that bedroom back there."

Megan.

Reluctant admiration fought his animosity, and lost. "Admit you stole the money. That'll make me respect you more."

"I can't confess to something I didn't do."

Frustration clawed through him. "Stop lying, Lana. Just…stop the lying."

She jumped off the stool. "I hope you choke on your food, Matthew Valente," she muttered, and raced out of the room.

Matt watched her leave, his appetite deserting him. He felt bad, but dammit, he'd done the right thing.

He had to remember—and keep on remembering—that his new wife might look like an angel,
but beneath that sweet facade she was as devious
as they come.

Three

After the way Matt had verbally attacked her last night, Lana hadn't expected to sleep soundly, but when she awoke the next morning she felt much more able to cope with being married.

And cope with Matt's attitude toward her, she decided, determinedly propelling herself out of bed. She had to get on with what life had dished out.

Megan was still asleep when Lana opened the connecting door. Lana's heart softened as she looked down at her child. Matt could think bad of her all he liked, and he could give her a hard time for the next year, but as long as Megan was safe, healthy and happy, she could withstand anything.

Even a charismatic womanizer like Matt Valente.

Pleased to have the time to shower without getting Megan sorted first, Lana returned ten minutes later dressed in tan slacks and a dark brown knit top, and found her daughter sitting up in her crib making noises and playing with her toys.

"There's Mummy's little darling." Giving her little girl a big kiss, she changed her diaper, then carried her to the kitchen to prepare her breakfast. She wasn't sure what was on the agenda today, if anything.

"You must be Mrs. Valente," a middle-aged woman said, coming forward to shake her hand as soon as they stepped into the large, airy kitchen.

Lana blinked at the name, then smiled. "Please call me Lana."

"Lana, then. I'm Ruth, your new housekeeper." She looked at Megan. "And this must be Megan. My, isn't she like her father?"

"I hope that's a good thing, Ruth," Matt said, coming into the kitchen and turning on the charm. He promptly leaned over and kissed Megan on the head.

Lana almost gasped. For a moment she thought he was going to kiss *her*. There was a knowing look in Matt's eyes as he moved away.

"Of course it is, Mr. Valente," Ruth said, pulling Lana back to the moment. "Now, breakfast will be served in the sunroom. What would the little one like?"

Lana told her, then watched in surprise as Matt took Megan from her arms and headed for the sunroom. She followed them, annoyed at his sheer arrogance.

"Excuse me," she hissed. "But do you have to do that?"

His brow rose. "What?"

"Take Megan off me like that. She's not a parcel, you know."

He slipped Megan into her high chair. "I thought I was helping. She's heavy."

"Yes, and I've managed to carry her around longer than you," she said pointedly.

His eyes hardened. "And whose fault is that?" he snapped, turning back to do up the strap. He fiddled with it, then muttered something under his breath. "How do you do this thing up?"

She shot him a look that said she was pleased he didn't know everything. "Like this. See."

He watched her show him. "You make it look so easy."

"That's because it's childproof."

One corner of his mouth twisted upward. "Are you trying to tell me something? No, don't answer that," he mocked, sitting down and reaching for the coffeepot. "So, what do you think of Ruth?"

She frowned while he poured her a coffee without asking. "She seems very pleasant and efficient."

"She comes highly recommended. She also has a degree in first aid and child care and has agreed to look after Megan while you're at work."

Lana stiffened. "You mean she'd be her *nanny*?"

He poured himself a coffee. "Yes."

"But Megan goes to day care already." She'd informed them it would only be for three days a week now instead of five, and Lana planned on spending those two other days with her daughter.

"I'm afraid that's not suitable anymore."

This set Lana's teeth on edge. "So I just move her because you snap your fingers?"

He put the coffeepot back, his mouth tightening. "This isn't about me. It's about our daughter."

She counted to five and then expelled a slow breath. "Look, don't you think with everything else new in her life it might be a good idea to keep some things the same?"

"Things can't stay the same, I'm afraid. Megan's a Valente now. Remember the press trying to take a picture of her after our wedding? Do you really want her at risk like that at the day care center? Or worse?"

Lana's heart jumped with fright. "Don't."

"This is only temporary. Once things settle down we'll try and find a day care center close by where we know she'll be safe, okay?"

She nodded, not sure she wanted to let her baby out of her sight ever again. She was just overreacting, of course, but she wanted Megan to have a normal life. Now that her daughter was recognized as a Valente, that would be impossible.

Just them, Ruth came into the room with a bowl of baby cereal. Lana thanked her then concentrated on feeding Megan, aware of Matt watching her.

"By the way," he said as she placed a spoonful of mush in Megan's mouth. "My mother has offered to look after Megan at any time, especially if we need to go out for an evening."

"That's good of her but I can't see it being necessary."

"There may be some events we can't avoid."

The spoon stopped midair. "Our marriage was to give your name to Megan. That's it." He'd made that more than clear, and she was more than happy with that.

"I don't like it either, but there are particular obligations that go along with being a Valente. Would you prefer I take another woman as my partner?"

The thought of him with other women had always made her feel sick to the stomach, but only because she'd wanted him so much herself. She'd hated being one of many.

And yet surprisingly she'd let him make love to her without a condom. She may have been slightly drunk, but somehow deep down she'd trusted him. It was crazy that she *still* trusted him in that respect.

She managed to school her features. "For Megan's sake, I wouldn't want you out and about with another woman, but that's your choice."

He swore softly. "Of course I'm not going to take another woman, but I wanted you to see how ridiculous the situation is. If I need someone to accompany me anywhere, then you're it, Lana. For Megan's sake," he reminded her.

The little girl in question started to babble and reach for the spoon in Lana's hand. "Sorry, pumpkin," she said, continuing to feed her.

When she turned back to look at Matt, he was pouring some muesli into a bowl and adding milk. She let his comment pass. Fine, so there were some things she would have to do as Matt's wife.

A few minutes later he pushed his empty bowl to the side. "There's a park around the corner. We should take Megan."

"A park? Today?" It was Saturday, but it was the last thing she expected he'd suggest the day after their wedding.

"Why not? The weather's supposed to be nice and the fresh air will do her good."

So he'd checked out the park as well as bought a new house? He'd been busy. If only he wasn't so involved...no, that was an idiotic thought.

"She would enjoy that," she said, and received a mocking look from him that *she* wouldn't.

Half an hour later, Lana gave Matt a quick lesson in changing diapers and dressing Megan in a playsuit, then she placed Megan in her stroller.

"I'll push it," Matt said, coming up behind her.

She was used to doing it herself. "No, that's okay."

"I don't mind."

She could see he wanted to do it, so she relented.

It was a funny feeling walking to the park with him. Never in a million years would she imagine her and Matt Valente together like this.

Married.

Parents.

Not lovers.

Once there, Matt looked like any proud father, pushing Megan on the swing, taking her down the slide, taking her on the small merry-go-round where he insisted Lana join them. A couple of times, she had to give herself a mental shake to stop believing this was real.

It was only real for him and Megan.

It wasn't real for them as a family.

A few yards along the small lake a man started tossing pieces of bread at the swans, who quickly began snapping it up. Suddenly Megan started to giggle.

Matt darted an amused glance at Lana. The man threw more bread and the swans ate it and Megan giggled louder. Her laughter was infectious and love rose in Lana's throat, not only for her little girl, but that she could share this moment with Matt.

It was a moment to treasure.

Suddenly Matt looked down at his daughter in his arms. "Oh God, she's gorgeous!" he said in awe, sending an odd tenderness through Lana.

"Yes, she is."

Their gazes touched for a brief moment before Megan began squirming in his arms and Matt turned away. "Come on," he said. "It's time to go."

Their morning was over.

Once back inside the house, Matt lifted Megan

out of the stroller and handed her to Lana without looking at her. "I'm going into the office. I have some work to catch up on. You and Megan will be fine here."

He left them to it and that smarted.

Clearly he had no idea she had her own workload to consider. She'd put in her resignation and now she had one week to tie up as many loose ends as she could. There was a ton of work to be done this weekend. Work she'd planned on doing whenever she got a spare moment.

Unlike Matt, who could just walk out the door and forget his obligations for a time.

She looked at Megan. "Well, pumpkin. It's just you and me again. Would you like the house tour?"

Megan stared at her.

"Right. The house tour it is," Lana said, refusing to let her irritation with Matt spoil the rest of her and Megan's day.

The one-level house was spacious and exuded elegance and style, encompassing every possible luxury. There were four bedrooms, one of which was Matt's, tempting her to peek inside but she decided not to.

There was a formal dining room she probably wouldn't use in their short married life, certain Matt would be careful about inviting anyone for dinner.

And she really loved the informal living room that allowed her to look out a wall of windows over a swimming pool and feature garden. She was especially pleased to see the pool was surrounded by the legally required child resistant fence.

It was a beautiful house, far different from the one she'd been raised in. Her parents' house had been moderate, but those four walls had shaken with yelling and abuse more often than not.

Shuddering, Lana put that to the side. This house was one she would be proud to own if her marriage had been a true one. As it was, she'd try to enjoy being here without letting herself get too attached to it.

Just as she wouldn't let herself get too attached to the Valentes.

For lunch, Ruth suggested Lana take Megan out on the patio in the sunshine. Megan played happily in the playpen they had set up beside the table, while Lana took the opportunity to unwind away from Matt's presence.

Half an hour later, Megan started getting cranky and Lana put her to bed. Thankfully she went straight to sleep.

Now it was work time for herself.

Quietly closing the connecting door between them, she kicked off her shoes and spread the paperwork out around her on the bed. No doubt Matt would want to use the study, and while she could, too, she'd be able to concentrate better in her own space.

Sunlight streamed through the window, making her sleepy. She continued to work until the warmth made her too tired to think. Perhaps she could take a quick power nap….

She shook herself awake. No, she needed to get this monthly report done. She couldn't let herself fall asleep. She needed this time while Megan was asleep or she'd have to stay up half the night working.

But that sunlight was so warm…so…

Something touched her shoulder and her eyes flew open to see Matt standing beside the bed. The sunlight had waned and shadows now darkened the room.

"Lana, it's almost dinnertime."

She sat up in a rush. "What? How?"

"Don't ask me questions I can't answer," he drawled.

She ignored that.

Good grief, had she really slept the afternoon away? "Where's Megan?"

"Ruth and I have been looking after her for the last couple of hours."

She ran her fingers through her hair. "Hours? I can't believe I didn't hear her crying."

"She was fine. I came home and she was playing happily in her crib. We've been in the living room getting to know each other. Then Ruth helped me bathe her and give her dinner. She'll be ready for bed soon."

Lana had the feeling that she was rapidly becoming "surplus to requirements" where her daughter was concerned.

"You've been working?" Matt asked abruptly, his gaze on the various papers and files.

She swung her legs over the edge of the bed and grimaced, more at herself than not. "I was *supposed* to be working, but I fell asleep before I got much of anything done."

His dark brows knitted together. "Why are you working on a weekend in the first place?"

Her lips tightened. Was it okay for him to work on a weekend and not her?

"I put my resignation in, remember? I've got a load of work to do before I leave."

"Surely they could get someone else to take over?"

"Eventually, but I don't like leaving them in the lurch." She pushed to her feet and smoothed her knit top down over her slacks. "At least after that sleep I'll be able to work late tonight."

"No."

She'd been about to step into her shoes, but the comment snapped her head up. "What did you say?"

"I said no. You've had a busy week. I don't want you working through the night."

Her growing anger cooled a little at his concern.

"And Megan needs a mother who's fit and healthy, not exhausted," he added, undoing the momentary good feeling she'd had toward him.

So this was about Megan again, not her. She didn't mind him being right about Megan needing a fit mother; he just wasn't right about *her.*

"You seem to have forgotten that *you* went into work today and *you're* Megan's father. Should I be questioning *your* fitness?"

His eyes reflected a glimmer of surprise; then he frowned. "How much work have you got?"

She glanced at the files on the bed. "A lot."

He remained quiet for a lengthy pause. "Okay, here's the deal. I'll look after Megan tomorrow if you take it easy tonight."

Her eyes widened. "*You'll* look after her?"

"I'll take her to my parents' place for a few hours, and then Ruth can help me when I get back. Deal?"

She thought about Matt sharing the responsibility for Megan's well-being. She'd been so used to doing everything herself that it took a second to rethink it.

All at once it hit her how much change this marriage would make to her life. When it had been just her and Megan, she'd been fully occupied with being responsible for every aspect of her daughter's life and juggling it with her own. Now she had no cooking, no cleaning, no food shopping, and nothing much to do each night at all. She certainly wouldn't have to sit down and work out the bills. In fact, she'd have plenty of time to spare.

And she'd have to learn to share her daughter. Coming to terms with that would take some time.

She looked up at Matt. "I'd appreciate all that, but I'll still need to work tonight to catch up." Their conversation at the breakfast table came to mind. "Unless you have other plans for us tonight?" As soon as the words left her mouth she felt herself blush. "I mean, we're not expected to go out or anything, are we?"

Derision entered his eyes. "No, we're not expected anywhere. I'll be going out myself after dinner anyway."

"Oh." Not wanting him to read her expression, she concentrated on putting on her shoes. "Then there should be no problem with me working tonight once she's down."

There was a moment's silence.

"Not one," he muttered, and left the room without waiting for her.

For a moment she sat back down on the bed, her heart constricting. Was he going to see another woman tonight? He'd said he wouldn't have any affairs for Megan's sake, but would he stick to that promise?

Could he?

Four

"Peekaboo!" Cesare said to the little girl sitting on his lap, and Megan giggled.

Matt watched his father in amusement. "You're such a pushover for a pretty face, Dad."

"How can I not be a pushover? She is so beautiful."

Matt felt himself swell with pride. He'd never been conscious of wanting his father's approval before, but it was a nice feeling knowing he had it now.

"He's a softie when it comes to his family, Matt," Isabel said, coming into the room with a small teddy bear in her hands.

"He's not the only, Mum," Matt said pointedly.

She smiled. "I'm allowed to spoil my grand-daughter."

Matt held up his hands. "Hey, don't let me stop you."

Isabel sat next to Cesare and waved the teddy bear in front of Megan's face. Megan immediately forgot the peekaboo game and reached for the stuffed animal. Matt laughed at the affronted look on his father's face.

Then Cesare turned to him, a sharpness in his eyes that had been there all along. "So the marriage is going well?"

Matt kept the smile on his face. "I've only been married two days, Dad."

Isabel tutted at her husband. "Give them time, Cesare."

Matt didn't set her straight. He hadn't told any of his family that the marriage was temporary, not even his parents. But they had to know he wasn't in love with Lana.

Thankfully Megan started to get a bit irritable just then, and Matt looked at his watch. "Speaking of time, Megan's due for her morning nap." He pushed to his feet, relieved to have something to do. "Here. Give her to me, Dad," he said, and scooped up his daughter.

Isabel stood, too. "Come on. I'll show you the spare room. We've put a crib in there for her."

Matt grinned wryly. "You haven't turned the room into a nursery, have you?"

His mother's lips twitched. "Not yet."

After that, Megan didn't wake up for a couple of hours, so it was mid-afternoon before he arrived back home.

Lana rushed out of the study when he opened the front door, taking Megan in her arms and fussing over her as if she'd been gone a week instead of a couple of hours.

"I've brought her back in original condition," he mocked, and wondered what it would be like if Lana fussed over *him*.

Don't go there.

"Is everything okay? No problems?" she asked, still frowning.

"Sorry to disappoint you. Not a one."

"Good." She suddenly had a smug look about her that set his antenna on high. "Because Ruth's gone to visit her sister in the hospital this afternoon and may not be back until late."

"So?" She obviously thought he couldn't handle his own daughter.

"Do you think you'll be able to look after Megan for the rest of the day?"

"Of course. We'll be fine."

"Oh." Her bubble burst. "Well, just call me if you need me."

Not on your Nellie, he mused, then noted the tired lines under her eyes. "How's the work going?"

"Moving along."

"You'd better get back to it, then."

"I'm here if you need me."

"We won't," he said, more snappish than he'd intended.

She handed Megan back, then headed for the study, but not before he saw her flinch. His jaw clenched. Why the hell was he feeling sorry for snapping at her? When all was said and done she'd had Megan to herself the last eleven months.

It was his turn now.

All at once the thought of her keeping Megan from him…of him possibly never knowing he had a daughter…never hearing his little girl giggle as he'd done with the swans yesterday…made his heart harden even more.

One thing was for sure. He wasn't going to rent out his old apartment now, after it had proven the perfect escape last night. He could always go out on the town, he supposed, but suddenly he didn't feel like it.

The rest of the afternoon was spent playing games with Megan on the living room floor, then letting her play with her toys while he sat down for a much-needed rest and a flick through the television channels with the remote to see what was showing.

The next minute her cry had him jumping to his feet. Quickly he scooped her up and checked her over, but she didn't appear to be hurt.

Maybe she was hungry? Yep, he could open a jar of baby food for her.

Only, it didn't soothe her.

Nothing did.

Lana appeared in the kitchen doorway. "Is every-thing okay in here?"

He looked up with a touch of relief. "I don't know. She won't stop crying and nothing I do will help."

Lana's brows drew together as she came forward, her gaze going over the little girl. "She's had a couple of big days. I think she's just overtired." She took the spoon out of his hand. "Come on, pumpkin. Let's eat this nice dinner, and then you can go to bed."

It sounded simple.

And it *was* simple when Lana did it, Matt mused, watching her in slight awe when half an hour later she finally put Megan down in her crib and the little girl shut her eyes and went to sleep.

"You've got a way with her," he murmured, step-ping back to allow her to leave the bedroom.

She pulled the door closed, then tipped her face up to him. "Not always."

Their eyes met.

Neither of them blinked.

They were standing very close and the scent of Valente's Woman stirred his nostrils—and his groin. If it had been any other woman he'd pull her up against him and make passionate love to her.

But not this woman.

This woman and passion mixed only too well.

His pulse thudding with thick desire, he pivoted before he could do something he regretted. "I think I'll go take a shower."

A long, cold shower.

Lana's heart raced as she watched Matt stride toward his bedroom and close the door behind him. For a minute there she thought he'd been about to kiss her. It had almost been the office Christmas party all over again.

Except neither of them had been drinking.

They'd been standing too close.

And she'd been feeling grateful for him taking care of Megan today.

And both of them were probably drained from the events of the past week, that's all.

Yes, that's all it was.

It couldn't be anything else. Matt blamed her for keeping his daughter from him. He thought she'd stolen money from him. He'd hate himself in the morning if he made love to her.

And she'd hate herself, too.

She'd have to make sure they didn't get too close in the future, she decided, making her way to the kitchen, where she put the casserole Ruth had left for them in the oven. She'd do another hour of work before dinner.

She'd just sat down at the desk when her cell phone rang. It was her boss, Mr. Wainwright.

A couple of minutes later she flung the study door open with steam coming out of her ears.

She couldn't believe it.

She *didn't* believe it.

How could a man who took such pride in his own work not expect she'd take pride in her work too?

Giving one quick knock, she stormed into Matt's bedroom. "How dare you!" she hissed, keeping her voice low so as not to wake Megan next door.

He frowned at her. "How dare I what?"

"You rang Mr. Wainwright! He says I don't have to finish up my week. He's releasing me from my contract early."

"And you've come to tell me you're grateful?" he joked.

"I can't believe you did this." Her lip curled. "On second thought, I can. The high-handed Valentes do what they like, when they like, and damn everyone else."

His jaw set. "As far as I'm concerned, if you want something you go and get it."

She flashed him a look of disdain. "What did you offer him? A bit of business thrown his way? You scratch my back and I'll scratch yours? Is that the way it is, Matt?"

A muscle pulsated in his cheek. "That's business."

She glared at him.

Glared for all she was worth until…

Something powerful drew her gaze downward.

And her eyes hit the hard contours of his chest.

His broad, *bare* chest.

All at once she realized he'd been in the middle of getting dressed and that his hand was still at the opening of his trousers. Her eyes flew back up to his face.

Zip.

He finished the job, sending the sound rushing through her veins, the blood rushing to her cheeks, but it was his knowing look that helped pull her together. He knew his half-dressed state had taken her off-guard. Knew he had made her knees go soft.

The arrogant devil!

She angrily gathered her thoughts. "My career is *none* of your business. And I mean that quite literally."

"I want you home with Megan."

She gasped, then bristled with indignation, forgetting all about his bare chest and the back scratching and the sexy sound of a zipper sliding up.

"You're not one of those men who don't want their wife to work at all, are you? Please tell me you don't want me pregnant and barefoot in the kitchen?"

His eyelids flickered and darkened. "Of course not. I meant this week, that's all. You said yourself she would find everything new and strange. I was just trying to make sure you spend some time with Megan until she gets used to it."

He was being caring of Megan? She believed that. But did he have to tread all over *her* to do it?

She set her chin in a stubborn line. "You could have asked me that yourself. But I suppose that's not worth your time. I'm still working three days a week with you. So don't try and renege on the deal, Matt."

"I don't renege on deals."

She stared at him. He seemed to have no idea he'd done anything wrong. Or more than likely he just couldn't acknowledge any wrongdoing.

"Don't interfere in my career again." She turned to leave the room.

"Lana?"

She stopped but didn't look back.

"Don't forget I'm your boss now. Your career both now and in the future is in my hands."

Lana swallowed. His tone was steel covered in velvet.

This time she did turn around. "Don't *you* forget something, Matt. I'm a Valente now. I can play dirty, too."

Then she turned on her heel and went back to the study, her mind spinning from the sheer arrogance of her new husband. If he thought he'd browbeat her, then he had another thing coming. She might no longer have a job to go to at Wainwright's, but she had a free day tomorrow before starting at Valente's. She would work her fingers to the bone to finish up as much as possible. It was a matter of pride, not to mention a small victory over Matt's attempt at controlling her.

Five minutes later she heard the front door close and Matt's car drive away. Evidently she'd be eating dinner alone tonight.

She told herself she was glad about that. She didn't want to break bread with a man who demanded she do what he wanted. A man who rode roughshod over everyone, and too bad for them if they didn't like it.

Yet she felt a chill. Memories of her father leaving the house for a night out on the town colored her thoughts. Where was Matt going? Who was he meeting? Would he come home smelling of alcohol? Of another woman? Dear Lord, she didn't think she could do this for a whole year.

At eleven she heard him return, heard his footsteps stop outside the study door, then she let out a slow breath as they continued on their way. That was exactly how she wanted it to stay, she told herself. She wanted to be just a small pause in his life until it was time for him to move on.

Five

Matt's face was shuttered when he walked into the sunroom the next morning, but Lana knew she flushed. She didn't want to think about her comment last night in his room on scratching backs, or the sound of a zipper going up or running her palms over his muscular chest, yet she couldn't seem to help herself.

She knew he saw it, too, and something reciprocal flashed in his brown eyes before he turned to focus on Megan.

He swung his gaze back to Lana.

"What do you plan for today?" he asked, surprising her with the question.

"Just a quiet day at home with Megan." No need

to tell him she planned on working until she'd finished her commitments to Wainwright's.

He stared for a moment. "Have a good day."

"I will."

He left not long after, and Lana roped in Ruth's help this one time to keep an eye on Megan, so by mid-afternoon she was able to take the paperwork over to Mr. Wainwright.

She felt such a sense of accomplishment as she handed over the files, but that soon disappeared on the way out when one of the female staff made a smart comment about her being lucky enough to marry Matt Valente.

Lana held her head high and ignored her. She wasn't feeling terribly lucky right now.

Far from it.

Arriving back at the house, she was disconcerted to see Matt's car in the driveway. She'd meant to ask Ruth not to say anything about today, but had forgotten in her rush to get out of the house.

Not that it really mattered if Matt knew what she'd been doing all day. Serve him right if he got a guilt attack from it. She pulled a face. Who was she kidding? Matt Valente didn't know the meaning of guilt.

She found him sitting on the leather sofa bouncing Megan on his lap, the pair of them laughing together. Her heart ached a little to join in the fun.

She stepped into the room. "You're home early."

His head turned to face her, the animation dying on his face. "I wanted to see Megan."

She felt as though she was intruding in something special.

As she was.

"Of course," she murmured, ready to leave them to it.

"Ruth said you'd gone to Wainwright's."

His words spun her back to face him. She shot him a defiant look. "Yes, I did. And I finished it all, despite your attempts to make me do otherwise."

"So I believe." A light of admiration entered his eyes. "Good for you."

His reply stunned her.

Then she quickly turned away, murmuring that she'd go change. She was confused and heartened in the same instant. Just when she wanted to hate him, he did or said something to make her change her mind.

Not that the feeling lasted long, she decided after dinner when he mentioned he was going out again, sluicing any softening toward him right down the drain.

Nonetheless, the next morning she was secretly glad of his company when they stepped out on the eighth floor of the House of Valente together. She wasn't actually nervous about it all, more uneasy. The real thief could still be here and could be watching her.

His middle-aged personal assistant greeted her warmly. "Lana, it's so nice to have you back."

"Thank you, Irene," she said, feeling cheered by the reception. She'd always enjoyed working here. Until her awareness of Matt had grown out of control.

Her eyes fell on Matt's office, and out of nowhere memories of the Christmas party came flooding back. She felt her cheeks begin to heat up, but thankfully the others didn't appear to notice.

Irene handed Matt a pile of messages. "You're late for your first appointment," she scolded in motherly fashion.

"I know, Irene, but we have a child who comes first now. Everyone else can wait." He turned to Lana, his eyes distant. "Irene will show you to your office." He turned and walked into his office and shut the door, leaving behind an awkward moment.

Typical.

Irene smiled at Lana. "New fathers are always cranky," she mused.

Lana forced a smile but said nothing. What could she say anyway? The press might have put a spin on their marriage being a love match, but it wouldn't take long before word got around the office once they saw her and Matt together. Loving they were *not*. Hopefully everyone would think they were just being private.

"Which office has he put me in, Irene?"

"The end one."

Lana got a sinking feeling in her stomach. "That's a single office, isn't it?"

"Yes, that's right. I'll show you. Then I'll take you around to meet the staff. There are some new faces."

Lana went with her, embarrassment and anger warring beneath the surface. Matt was certainly making sure she started off on the wrong foot with her co-workers.

Of course that wasn't hard to do with Evan Rogers, one of the other accountants, whom she'd worked with before. He was so swarmy that if she suspected anyone of stealing money, it was him.

"Lana, how lovely to see you back," he gushed at her in front of the others. "And you've got the end office now, too. How…fortunate."

Lana kept the smile on her face and ignored his dig. She actually hoped it *was* Evan who'd stolen the money. No one else deserved to go to jail like he did, she mused, determining that Evan's accounts would be a great place to start investigating. He might not have been stupid enough to take money that led straight back to him, but perhaps he'd made a minor mistake somewhere…anywhere….

After that she managed to focus as she got reacquainted with the financial aspects that concerned her job, and by late morning she felt right at home. The work was so familiar she could do it with her eyes shut, though she knew that therein lay the danger. She had to keep her eyes open for any sign of fraud. Not just by Evan but by anyone else. She would bide her time; it might look strange if she started looking up old accounts straightaway. She would do that once she felt able to without suspicion.

She didn't see Matt until he came to get her to go home.

"How was your first day back with us?" he said, leaning against the doorjamb.

He looked gorgeous and noticing it made her angry with herself. And damn, but she was still angry with him anyway.

Her mouth tightened. "You shouldn't have given me this office."

His eyes narrowed. "Why?"

"I didn't have one by myself before. I shared with three others."

"You weren't my wife before."

"Exactly. You shouldn't show me any favoritism." She only just refrained from saying that perhaps he should share that particular point with the others instead of ignoring her as he had all day, but then it sounded as though she actually *wanted* him to spend time with her.

"Maybe I should put you in my office with me," he quipped, his lips curving sensually.

Her heart jumped in her throat. "I hope you're kidding."

All at once his smile disappeared and his face shuttered up. "Obviously," he muttered, straightening. "Are you ready to leave?"

"Give me a moment to finalize something and I'll be with you."

"I'll go talk to Irene until you're ready."

She nodded, glad for him to take his presence out of her sight. If only he could take the memories of being in his office with him. Maybe coming back here wasn't a good idea after all.

No, she had to prove to Matt that the mother of his child wasn't a thief. It was important to her.

She said nothing more in the car, but she was glad when they arrived home and she got to kiss and cuddle Megan. She missed her little girl when she went to work, though she knew she'd miss her work if she stayed home all day, too. She had the best of both worlds right now. It was one of the positive things about this situation.

Matt insisted on feeding Megan again that night, and with Ruth around the atmosphere was quite jovial.

Then he went to take a phone call and Lana put Megan in the bath, laughing at her little girl splashing the water with her toy duck.

Megan thought her mother laughing was funny and she splashed the water with her duck again, only this time the water splashed on Lana's knit top.

"Megan! Look what you've done to Mummy," Lana said, chuckling, not minding in the least getting wet.

Splash.

"Ooh, you little devil," she said, and gently splashed the water so that it slapped against her daughter's belly.

Megan giggled, then splashed the water again. Lana returned the favor.

"You two look like you're having fun."

Lana's head swung to the doorway. The smile froze on her lips. "Er…she likes her bath time."

"You look like you do, too." His eyes dropped to her wet top, his pupils dilating before he lifted his gaze back to her face. "Keep playing. I like watching."

Lana's breath hitched. She dared not look down, but she was sure her nipples were beaded and easily seen, and after that glance of his she almost expected to see steam come off her clothes.

She swallowed. "No, she's finished her bath. It's time for bed."

Lana took the toy duck out of Megan's hands and went to pick her up, but before she could the little girl made an outraged sound and hit the water with her fist, then stuck her bottom lip out in an angry pout.

Something in her expression looked so much like Matt at that moment, Lana could only exclaim, "Lord, she's the image of *you*."

He looked startled. "Actually I was just thinking how much she was like you."

It was her turn to be surprised. She didn't think her daughter had any of her features and she was pleased.

But a pout?

"I don't pout," she said with a rueful grin.

The corners of his mouth quirked upward. "Well, I certainly don't."

They stared at each other, and Lana felt her smile slip. He turned and left the room.

Swiftly she turned back to Megan and concentrated on getting her ready for bed. And when she sat down to dinner, it was alone. Matt had already gone out.

At work the next day Lana was placing some reports on Irene's desk when Cesare called to her from inside Matt's office. She frowned as she stepped up to the doorway.

"Come in, Lana." He got to his feet and came to give her a kiss on the cheek, making her feel like one of the family. "Welcome back, *cara*."

She wasn't used to such affection. Her parents had been too full of hatred for each other to have anything left over for friendliness.

"Thank you, Cesare." She didn't look at Matt, nor did she let her thoughts show on her face.

Cesare led her to one of the chairs. "Sit down here." He waited until she did, then went back to his own seat. "I was just telling Matt that his mother and I have ballet tickets at the Opera House for Friday night."

Lana eased into a smile. Now, *this* was a nice safe subject. "How lovely."

"Do you like the ballet, Lana?"

"Love it," she said with enthusiasm. She'd only ever been once, but she—

"Then you and Matt can go in our place."

She darted a look at Matt, then back at her

father-in-law. "I…we couldn't possibly take your tickets, Cesare."

"You would be doing us a favor, Lana. Both Izzie and I have a full day on Friday and we'll be just too tired to go out that night, as well. And the friends who gave us the tickets would be insulted if we didn't use them."

"But—"

"Thanks, Dad." Matt cut across her. "We'll be happy to take them off your hands."

Lana's eyes snapped back to Matt, but her glare bounced off him.

"Good. Your mother and I will look after Megan."

Lana tensed as she turned to Cesare. "Won't she be too much for you both after such a long day?"

"She's our granddaughter. She'll never be too much."

Her heart did a roll. "That's sweet of you, Cesare, but—"

"No problem, Dad." Matt cut across her again. "That'll work out just fine. We'll be able to enjoy ourselves knowing Megan is being looked after so well."

Cesare nodded with satisfaction. "Good. Your mother said to say that you should leave Megan with us for the night. That way you won't have to worry about waking her up and taking her home again. It would only unsettle her." With that bombshell, the older man stood up. "I must get back home now. I just dropped by to see how things were going here."

"Business is booming, as you well know," Matt teased.

Cesare kissed her cheek, and Lana barely waited for him to close the door behind him to get her words out. "Damn you, Matt. You shouldn't have accepted."

"I didn't have much of a choice. I don't want him to overdo things by going to too many events. And he will accept the invitation himself if we don't go."

"Wouldn't Nick or Alex like the tickets? I'm sure Sasha or Olivia would jump at the chance of going to the ballet."

"They've already made plans they can't break."

Her lip curled. "Do you know that for a fact, or are you just guessing?"

He nodded at the telephone. "Call them and see. My brothers are attending a charity dinner on Friday. I'd already gotten out of that one, but I didn't expect this."

Okay, so she could accept that. "He's matchmaking, you know."

"You may not have noticed but we're already married," he mocked.

"He's still matchmaking."

All at once his eyes closed in on her. "*Now* I see where this is coming from. You're worried about being alone in the house with me all night." He paused. "You have nothing to worry about, Lana."

"That's obvious," she said before she could stop herself.

He pinned her with a stare. "What does that mean?"

She realized she had to tread carefully. She didn't want him thinking she cared. "Just that you've been spending a lot of time out each night."

His look sharpened. "Do you have a problem with that?"

She raised one slim shoulder. "Not at all. It was just an observation."

Seconds crawled by.

"Do you think I'm with another woman?"

"Are you?" she challenged, despite not being sure she was ready to hear this.

A pulse beat in his lean cheek. "Perhaps I might just be trying to stick to the deal we made about separate lives. It doesn't necessarily mean I'm out with other women."

Silly relief raced through her veins but she quickly held it at bay. Was he just telling her what he wanted her to know? "I'm glad to hear it. For Megan's sake, of course."

"Of course." His eyes held hers, then flicked over her tailored business suit. "Do you have anything to wear Friday night? If not, get yourself something and charge it to me. As a matter of fact, you'll need a new wardrobe anyway."

Her back went rigid. "I don't need any clothes and I definitely don't need your money. I can afford to buy myself something if I need it."

"I don't want my wife walking around in department store clothes."

Her pride felt bruised. Not all her clothes were

off the rack. This suit certainly wasn't. She liked nice clothes as much as the next woman and sometimes she found real bargains.

She angled her chin at him. "There's nothing wrong with department store clothes."

"I didn't say there was. I just don't want my wife walking around in them." She went to speak and he held up his hand. "Do you really want to be the only one wearing cotton instead of silk?"

"Do you really think I care?"

He scrutinized her response, brows drawn together. "No, I don't think you do."

Her stomach fluttered.

"You're lucky, Lana. You've got style. You could wear cotton and make it look like silk anyway."

She gave the softest of gasps, then held her breath, knowing she had to keep this on a professional level.

"Then it won't matter if I wear department store clothes, will it?" Not waiting for an answer, she quickly stood up.

There was a moment's pause before he muttered throatily, "Wear what you want."

"I will." Suppressing a shiver of trepidation, she walked to the door and didn't stop until she reached her office, putting some distance between them.

Had she misheard that low pitch to Matt's voice back there?

Or had it been wishful thinking on her part?

She prayed *not*.

For either thing.

* * *

"Anything good on television tonight?" Matt asked, plopping down on the living room sofa later that day.

Lana had been watching the end of a current affairs program and now she looked up in shock. "You're staying in?"

"You would prefer me to go out?" he drawled.

"No." She looked back at the television. "No, it will be nice to have some company," she admitted, not realizing until this moment how lonely she'd felt each evening.

And that didn't make sense. She'd always enjoyed her own company, so why was she feeling lonely when nothing really had changed?

"What's on tonight?" Matt asked, interrupting her thoughts.

"Um…I was going to watch a movie after this."

"A chick flick?" he said with something like disgust.

She had to smile. "No, not a chick flick. It's a spy film."

His gaze rested on her lips a moment; then he turned to the television. "Death and mayhem. That's more like it."

Lana swallowed hard, her mind racing. That low pitch had been in his voice again, the way it had today in his office. Oh, she didn't think he was planning any type of seduction. She had no doubt he was as determined to keep their marriage as platonic as she was.

So why was her trepidation increasing? More importantly, why was her heart thudding with growing excitement? Hadn't she learned her lesson at all?

The tension in her shoulders relaxed. Her comment about him going out every night must have found its mark.

Yes, that's all it was.

A few minutes later the movie began and for a little while she even managed to forget about Matt's presence, until there was a break and he started talking about a review he'd read some time ago.

Trying to appear nonchalant, Lana responded but she wasn't actually listening. Another part of her was watching his velvet brown eyes, down to those firm lips, over the shadow of his jaw darkened by the end of day, to the bob of his Adam's apple cushioned by that strong throat.

All of him.

Her gaze traveled back up to his eyes, and she swallowed hard at the awareness in them.

He knew.

Thankfully the movie came back on and she dragged her gaze away until the next break when she decided she couldn't sit still any longer.

"Would you like some coffee?" she asked, jumping to her feet. "And some cake. Ruth did some baking today."

"That sounds good." He unfurled from his chair and stood up, too. "I'll go check on Megan while you do that."

They went their separate ways and in the kitchen Lana came up for air. Heavens, she felt like such a novice. Her face was giving away her thoughts as if she were handing them to Matt on a platter.

Oh, look, Matt. I'm hot for you tonight. I need you to make love to me. Come and take me.

She smiled grimly. Maybe someone would come and take her—away. And they should lock her up until she had her head examined for wanting a man who would never commit to any woman.

Ten minutes later they were eating cake and drinking coffee, and she was feeling very proud of herself for focusing back on the movie instead of on Matt.

"You've dropped some cream on you," he muttered.

The spoon stopped halfway to her mouth. "I did? Where?"

"There."

She looked down to her cleavage, where a blob of cream had fallen. She could feel her cheeks redden. Quickly she scooped it up and licked it off her finger.

"You've left some." He leaned forward with his napkin. "Here. Use this."

She waved it aside. "That's okay. I've got a napkin around here somewhere."

"Use this," he all but growled, and she looked up and saw a hot flash in his eyes that said he'd lick the cream off himself if she didn't hurry up and do it.

Her pulse skittered as if it were on an icy road.

Hastily she found her napkin. "Look, I've found it," she exclaimed, holding it up. She wiped the spot, then gave an awkward smile. "This cake is so nice, isn't it?"

A nerve pulsed near his temple. "Very nice."

Flushing, she turned back to the television. The air throbbed with painful sensuality between them, but somehow she got through to the end of the movie.

As soon as it ended, a starter pistol went off in her mind, but she pretended to yawn oh so casually. "I guess I'd better go to bed," she said, slowly pushing to her feet when all she wanted to do was run to the door.

"Me, too." He flicked the remote and turned off the television. "I'll just make sure everything's locked up first."

Her gaze slid to him. "Well, good night. See you in the morning."

There. That was a warning.

Do not disturb.

A moment crept by, then, "See you tomorrow."

There was a clipped sound to his voice and she breathed a sigh of relief as she hurried to her room to take a shower. Not that she expected Matt would come after her. The danger had been back there in the living room.

Half an hour later she lay in bed wide-awake. She couldn't settle. Her room felt claustrophobic and her pulse was still jumpy from being in Matt's company all evening. She needed to get up and move around, do anything but lie here and think of things best left alone.

She didn't bother putting her bathrobe on over her short, satiny chemise; she figured Matt would have gone to bed.

All was quiet as she opened her door and padded along the plush carpet to the living room, moonlight guiding the way. She could see the lights from the swimming pool casting shadows ahead and—

"What are you doing?"

She gasped and whirled around. Matt had come up behind her in the doorway. "Oh, you frightened me!"

There was a tiny pause. "You're supposed to be in bed," he said, making it sound as if she'd gone back on her word.

"Er…I couldn't sleep." She noticed he was still in the same clothes. "You're supposed to be in bed, too," she said, almost accusingly.

"I'm on my way there now."

It sounded like an invitation.

She moistened her mouth. "Well, I must go." She went to hurry past him. She'd been unwise to come out here in her night wear.

He caught her by the arm. "Next time put on a robe," he rasped, holding her still, his touch sending little zings of full awareness through her bare skin.

He let her go.

She hurried to her room and leaned back against

the door, her heart thudding beneath her breast. Oh Lord. The danger wasn't so much back there in the living room.

The danger was in herself.

Six

The next day Lana decided it was time to do some investigating. Now that she was part of the furniture, she could blend in more easily and be a bit more adventurous in her search for the truth.

But she waited until Matt came into her office to take her home before saying anything. "I'm going to stay back here for a couple of hours tonight."

He sent her an exasperated look. "It's a waste of time if you ask me."

"I'm not asking you, Matt." She was getting nowhere with clearing her name. She had to do something. "If you could put Megan to bed, I'd appreciate it." This once she would have to miss seeing her daughter. Heck, the main reasons she was doing this was for Megan.

He scowled. "What time will you be home?"

"I don't know. Eight, perhaps. I'll catch a taxi."

"I don't like it."

"Really."

"I'll come back and get you at seven. Ruth can look after Megan."

"But—"

"No buts. I'll be here at seven."

She took one look at his hard features and knew he wasn't going to budge. "Okay, but not before seven. I want a chance to actually get some work done." She didn't mention anything else out loud, in case the walls had ears.

Matt turned and left, and Lana took a deep breath. Right. Now she could concentrate without his skepticism in her face.

An hour later the whole floor was quiet, and after doing a check that everyone had gone, she was focusing intensely on the reports on her computer screen when Evan popped his head around the door.

"What are you doing here so late?" he asked, making her jump.

"Oh, Evan! You frightened me." She caught her breath. "Anyway, I could ask you the same question."

"I had to go see someone on the next floor." He stepped into the office. "Can I help you with anything?"

Inside she was panicking, but outside she

casually clicked on her screen saver, then leaned back on her chair. "Not, not really. I'm just catching up."

He frowned. "You were always on top of things before."

"These days I'm a married woman with a child."

He looked at her strangely, then he smiled a false smile. "Let me know if you need any help."

"I will."

Like hell.

"I'm going home now. Good night, Lana."

"Good night."

He left, but she didn't move for long moments. It wasn't until she heard the whisper of the elevator door closing that she let herself relax. Then she unlocked her computer screen and started searching the reports again.

At seven, Matt returned. "Find anything?" he said from the doorway.

"No." She hated to admit it.

"I told you."

She couldn't let herself be beaten. "I'm close to finding something. I can feel it."

He eyes said he didn't believe it. "Grab your things and I'll take you home."

His attitude shouldn't have disappointed her, but it did. She tidied her desk and picked up her handbag. "By the way," she said on the way to the elevator. "I've decided to work tomorrow. Ruth won't mind looking after Megan for the day, too."

He raised a brow, his eyes hardening. "Don't you think this is going too far?"

"No."

He shrugged. "Your choice."

"Yes, it is."

"Can you send this out by courier please, Irene?" Lana said, holding out some paperwork.

Irene picked up her ringing telephone, but nodded at one of the trays on her desk. "Just put it in that pile so Matt can check it first."

Lana frowned as the other woman turned away to deal with the person on the other end of the line. Her heart sank. Was this procedure something new? Or was this just for *her*?

She waited for Irene to finish her call.

"Does Matt check everyone's work now?" she asked as casually as she could.

Irene bit her lip. "Oh dear. Lana, he's just looking out for you. I told him he was being overprotective, but I guess it comes with being married now."

How she managed to keep a straight face right then, Lana didn't know. Here she was, working hard to clear her name, and all he cared about was keeping an eye on her in case she stole his precious money. Oh, how she wished she could come clean about Dan buying the apartment. She'd love to see the shock on Matt's face.

She grimaced inwardly. Unfortunately, then he'd be asking her where the fifty thousand dollars went.

And when she couldn't tell him—she was innocent, after all—he'd start investigating her background more than he'd evidently done already. And then Dan's private life would be at risk of being leaked to the newspapers.

No, she couldn't let that happen.

"You may be right, Irene," she said, and went back to her office, running into Evan along the way. The man had a knowing look in his eyes that set her blood boiling again. For Irene to know that Matt was checking her work was totally humiliating. But for Evan to know, and possibly the others—it made her want to sink right through the floor.

Unable to sit still a moment more, she strode back down the corridor. Irene was nowhere to be seen, but she wouldn't have cared anyway. This was between her and her husband.

Through the open door, she could see the man in question sitting at his desk. Without pause she stepped inside his office and shut the door behind her.

He looked up as she approached the desk.

"Damn you, Matt."

He put down his pen and leaned back in his leather chair, looking very much the employer. "I'm sure you're going to tell me what the problem is."

She hated his complacency. "This is the second time this week you've gone over my head."

"And this is the second time you've stormed into a room uninvited."

A picture of her storming into his bedroom came to mind, but she shook it off. He was just trying to knock her off balance because he knew he was in the wrong here.

"You've been checking all my work. You've embarrassed me greatly, Matt."

"As opposed to being embarrassed if one of the others found you stealing money?" he derided.

She drew a sharp breath. "I *didn't* steal anything."

"Prove it."

"I will when I get a chance, but you're undermining me. If the real thief thinks you're checking my work, then he might suspect we know the money is missing. He might realize that you're blaming me. And then he'd have to know I'm trying to prove my innocence."

Matt got to his feet and came around the desk. "How do you know it's a he?"

She was taken aback. Was he actually beginning to believe her?

She lifted her shoulders. "I *don't* know. It may not be a man. I was just assuming it might be."

He stopped right in front of her. "Don't assume anything, Lana. It could get you into trouble."

She frowned. "What's that supposed to mean?"

"Assuming can be dangerous." A purposeful gleam appeared in his eyes, his tone silky. "Like last night for instance. When I saw you in that short nightgown I could have assumed you wanted me to make love to you."

She caught her breath. "I wasn't…I didn't…"

"Didn't you?"

"No! I can't believe you thought—"

He fastened his mouth on hers and for a stunned second everything held still. Then his firm lips began to move. Her heart kick-started again just as his tongue slipped inside and took command.

Her legs buckled at the intimacy. She wanted to pull away, not to let him have such control over her, but the incomparable richness of his tongue on hers was a lure she couldn't resist.

He wrenched his mouth away.

And suddenly it was over.

He let her go.

"Next time you storm into my office," he growled, "*this* is what you'll get."

She was at a loss for words.

Lost for want of him.

His eyes burned into her. "And heaven help you if you ever storm into my bedroom again like you did Sunday night."

Panic stirred in her chest, but she somehow subdued it.

She pulled her shoulders back. "For the record I did not go out in my nightgown to seduce you," she said icily. "And for the record I did not steal any money."

She spun on her heel and left him to it, vaguely aware of her brother-in-law Nick coming out of the elevator and saying hello, as she muttered a reply and swept past him to her office. Right now she wasn't feeling too kindly to any Valente.

Her hands were shaking by the time she got back to her desk. Oh God. That kiss had shot down all her hard-earned defenses. And now, somehow, she had to scramble to put them up again.

"Now, that's one pretty pissed off lady," Nick drawled, entering Matt's office.

Matt schooled his features and returned to his chair, silently cursing himself. "Mind your own business, Nick."

"Hmm. Touchy, are we?"

"No." He watched Nick park himself on the chair opposite. Damn him. Brothers could be such a pain at times, and *his* brothers in particular. They always thought they were right.

Nick's mouth quirked. "You know, Matt. I haven't told you this before but I find something really funny."

Okay, he'd bite.

"What?"

"I find it hilarious that after Alex and I warned you about Dad's plan to make you marry, you ended up doing it to yourself."

"Shut up, big brother."

It took a moment for the amusement to leave Nick's face. His eyes sharpened as he seemed to realize this was more than serious. "What's the problem?"

Matt winced. Okay, so his brothers liked to tease,

but they were always concerned for his welfare. "Sorry. It's not a good time to be discussing my personal life right now."

"So things really aren't going well between you and Lana?"

"Let's say they could be better."

Nick considered that. "Sasha and I had some rough patches, too. Not in the bedroom, mind you. We always seem to be communicable on that level." He looked at Matt speculatively. "Oh, hell. You two haven't slept together, have you?"

Matt's mouth twisted. "We did once. It's how Megan came to be here."

Nick waved a dismissive hand. "I mean since you've been married."

"No."

"Then there's your problem."

He shook his head. "We've got more problems than sex, Nick."

"Such as? You've got a beautiful wife and daughter. A great house, a good job, terrific brothers—well, at least one," he joked.

Matt ignored the last bit.

He looked sourly at his brother. "Don't you have an office of your own to go to?"

Nick gave a quiet chuckle. "No wonder Lana can't put up with you. You're a grouch."

"And you've outstayed your welcome," Matt pointed out, grateful for his concern but equally grateful he was letting the subject drop.

"Okay, I'll leave. I only came to give you some good news. Valente's Woman is a finalist in the Fragrance of the Year Award."

Matt felt a rush of pleasure. "That's terrific. Dad will be so proud."

"You bet. Alex asked Dad to come down to the office. We'll open a bottle of bubbly." Nick pushed to his feet and headed for the door. "See you in about fifteen minutes?"

"Fine."

Nick stopped briefly. "By the way, Matt. That's a nice shade of lipstick you're wearing."

Matt smiled grimly at the parting shot even as thoughts of Lana returned.

Hell.

If he wasn't careful he'd be making love to her again and then they'd be right back where they started. And if that happened, for all her talk to the contrary, she might even want to make this marriage permanent.

Not a chance.

He might want her physically more than he'd ever wanted any woman, but that didn't mean he was ready to be tied down. This marriage was only temporary, and if she tried to make it permanent, then she was in for a shock.

No way.

Getting up from his chair he went into the bathroom. Sure enough, he had a smear of Lana's peach-tinted lipstick on his top lip.

And the soft honeyed taste of her in his mouth.

* * *

Lana was relieved when Matt went out that evening after dinner. There'd been a hint of danger in his eyes ever since this afternoon. That kiss had shaken her, and it seemed it had shaken him, too. They were both in deep trouble.

Together they were an explosive combination. If she wasn't careful there'd be nothing left but to pick up the pieces. She'd done that once before. She wasn't sure she could do it again.

So she wasn't sure why she went out the next day and bought herself a new dress for the ballet that evening. It wasn't just to cheer herself up. Nor was it because her money worries were nonexistent right now and she could afford silk instead of cotton.

Could it be that she *wanted* Matt to be proud of being seen with her? Okay, it was a very feminine reaction. She could admit that.

And so was defiance, she thought, somewhat smugly as she stepped into the living room that evening and saw Matt standing at the windows with Megan in his arms, looking out at the swimming pool.

He turned around when he heard her.

And that dangerous gleam stirred.

"Is that a new dress?"

She smoothed the front of the peacock-blue material over her stomach in a nervous gesture. "Yes."

"Did you charge it to me?"

That brought her chin up. "No."

His eyes swept over her, trickling down her form

like a soft powder. "You look lovely," he said, his voice a touch husky.

Her throat went dry. She wasn't used to such compliments from Matt. She feared she could get used to it.

"Thank you." She moistened her mouth, wanting to say how nice he looked himself, but that would have been an understatement. In his dark suit and white shirt, he was sex appeal personified, his sophistication imprinted on him like a birthmark.

The Valente birthmark.

Thankfully Megan babbled something, and not for the first time Lana was grateful for her daughter's presence.

They drove to Cesare and Isabel's apartment and dropped Megan off for the night, the older couple delighted to have their grandchild and neither looking the least bit exhausted.

"Your father seems to have weathered his day well," Lana said pointedly, once they were in the car and heading toward the city center.

"Don't let him fool you. He's good at hiding things."

Cesare wasn't the only one, Lana pondered, stealing a look at Matt's profile, then turning away when he caught her gaze. He looked so handsome he quite took her breath away.

In what seemed like moments, they were parking the car in the Opera House car park. He cupped her elbow as they walked to the elevator that would take them up to the concourse area, but she broke contact with him when they stepped around a crowd of people chatting.

"We might run into some people I know," he said in a clipped tone, cupping her elbow again. "So do you think you could look like you actually want to be with me?"

She tried to ignore the tingle of his touch. "You don't have to put on a show tonight, Matt. Everyone must have figured out by now why you married me."

"I don't give a damn what everyone thinks they know, but I do have some pride. You're a beautiful woman and they would expect that we're having a physical relationship."

"Then they'd be wrong," she said, but her mind was on his comment.

He thought her beautiful.

Just as quickly another thought replaced it.

He also thought her a thief.

They went straight to their seats. As the dance started, she got caught up in the stirring power of the ballet. The superb music accompanying the emotional tale wowed her until she forgot all about her problems and Matt beside her.

Until intermission arrived. The curtain lowered and she felt his eyes upon her.

"You're enjoying yourself?"

It was silly to feel a bit self-conscious. "Yes, very much."

"Good. My father will be happy."

She was glad she could make *someone* happy.

She stood up. "I think I'll go find the ladies' room."

He got to his feet, too. "I'll meet you in the bar."

They parted ways not long after and once she'd finished in the ladies room, she was walking along the corridor to the bar when she saw a wallet on the floor.

Automatically she picked it up and gasped when she saw the wad of hundred-dollar bills inside. The name "Arthur Taran" was on the driver's license. She was about to go hand it into management when she caught sight of one of the staff. She gave it to her instead and the woman promised she'd find the owner.

Lana soon forgot about it on reaching the bar and finding Matt talking with a debonair young couple around his own age. He handed her a drink of wine and introduced them as Justin and Sara.

"So you're Lana," Sara said warmly. "I saw your wedding picture in the paper and thought you looked beautiful, but it didn't do you nearly enough justice."

Lana immediately liked the other woman. "And I was having a bad day, too," she said with a wry smile.

They all laughed, including Matt, whose smile made her heart skip a beat, even with that slight hardness in the back of those eyes.

Sara turned to Matt. "Matt, she's not only beautiful but has a sense of humor. And I bet she's a really nice person."

"Would I have married anyone who wasn't?" Matt drawled.

"If she was beautiful, yes!" Justin joked, then winked at Lana. "I went to school with him."

Lana smiled. "You clearly know him well."

Sara laughed, then, "Oh, I'm so glad we ran into each other."

A short time later it was time to return to their seats.

"Let's come back here and have a drink afterward," Sara suggested. "We don't have to rush back home tonight. Justin's parents are looking after our little boy."

"Sounds good," Matt said, drawing a glance from Lana, but his face gave nothing away.

On the way back to their seats he didn't clarify whether she wanted to have a drink afterward with his friends. Not that she minded spending time with them. It was preferable to going home and knowing it was only her and Matt alone in the house.

Just the two of them.

She winced inwardly. There was nothing to worry about. She and Matt would have that drink, then go home and go to their separate rooms, just as they did every night.

And just because Matt kissed her in the office yesterday, and just because now there was an increasing awareness between them, didn't mean a thing. She would concentrate on enjoying the ballet. And then she'd enjoy his friends.

And that would be that.

The curtain lifted and the performance continued, and Lana became absorbed in the movement once again.

After the ballet had finished to much-deserved applause, they met up with Sara and Justin in the bar, where the other couple had found a secluded table near a window that gave an amazing night view of Sydney Harbour.

"Do you enjoy the ballet, Lana?" Sara asked, once everyone was seated. "It's ages since I've been."

"I haven't been to the ballet since I was twelve," Lana admitted. "My mother brought me as a treat for my birthday." She sighed. "She's gone now."

Sara reached out and squeezed her arm. "I'm sure it's a memory you treasure."

Lana warmed to her even more.

"Here she is, Mr. Taran. This is the lady who found your wallet."

Lana looked up to see the staff member to whom she'd given the lost wallet, and an older gentleman standing by their table.

He pumped Lana's hand. "My dear, thank you so much for returning my wallet."

Lana smiled. "It was my pleasure, Mr. Taran."

"I'd like to give you a reward."

She waved that aside. "No, but thank you for offering."

"No, thank *you*." His smile encompassed the others then he walked away.

"See, I told you she was nice," Sara said, but

Lana was aware of Matt watching her with an odd look in his eyes.

She ignored him and actually began to relax and enjoy herself as she talked about kids with Sara, watched Justin joke with Matt about being a new father, and generally had a good time over two glasses of wine.

An hour later she felt warm and even pleasant toward Matt and he even seemed to be more relaxed around her.

He really was a heartbreaker, she mused, peeking beneath her lashes at him, caught out with a knowing look that glinted on the verge of hot. Yet suddenly she didn't seem to care. The wine was making her feel good.

"I think it's time we let these two lovebirds go home to bed, Justin," Sara said, then yawned delicately. "Besides, I need my beauty sleep."

The words made Lana wince. Was she really looking like a lovesick idiot? Or was Sara seeing more than there was?

Definitely.

She wasn't in love with Matt. She wanted him, certainly. He made her ache for him physically, but that had nothing to do with affection.

Everyone agreed to meet up soon, then Matt put his hand on her elbow as he walked her back to their car.

Thankfully the night air kept her head clear.

"You handed in that wallet," he said, once they were in the car, his eyes inscrutable.

"It was the right thing to do."

"You weren't tempted to keep it?"

She met his eyes without flinching. "No."

She hadn't handed in the wallet to get his approval, but it would have been nice for him to acknowledge her honesty.

"No one would have known," he pointed out.

"*I* would have known."

He studied her and an odd expression flickered across his face before he turned away to start the engine. "My friends really like you."

"And that surprises you?"

"Not at all. You're very charming."

So was he.

Except with *her*.

"I gather you're happy with my performance tonight, then?" she said with an underlying note of sarcasm.

"Performance?"

"They think we're happily married."

He glanced at her only briefly. "It'll do."

She sighed with frustration and left him to concentrate on the driving. It didn't matter what she did, his opinion of her wasn't going to change. He wanted to think bad of her and he would continue on that path.

So why on earth had she been worried about spending the night alone in the house with him? He'd kissed her in his office to punish her, not because he'd had an overpowering need to feel her lips beneath his.

Not the way she did his.

All at once he cast her a sideways glance, and his gaze dropped to her mouth and darkened. "Don't," he growled, before returning to the road.

Startled, she felt her thoughts fumbling to catch up to him. Then she realized. Until that moment she hadn't been aware of touching her mouth with her fingertips, remembering him there.

The mouth that he had kissed.

Heavens.

Had she given herself away?

The tension was palpable for the rest of the journey, but Lana didn't know how to disperse it. The two of them seemed to create a sexual energy together that was multiplied by the confines of the car.

It made her skittish and eager to get home so she could hide in her room.

Yes, hide.

Somewhere that she wouldn't be tempted to make love to him. She was a coward and she could admit it.

They arrived home shortly after, but he surprised her by parking the car near the front door and not in the garage. Was he going out again?

To another woman?

She felt a moment's squeezing pain. Wasn't it unrealistic of her to believe he could remain celibate? It wasn't as if they had a love match. He was a virile man.

She avoided his eyes until they were inside.

"Lana?"

The intensity in his voice trapped her where she stood.

"Look at me, Lana."

Her heart bumped her ribs into action. She swung toward the kitchen. "Coffee. Do you want—"

"*You.*" He caught her by the waist and smoothly put her up against the wall. "That's what I want."

She swallowed hard. "Matt, in the car, if you think I was—"

"Oh, you were." His eyes zeroed down to her mouth. "You were thinking of our kiss."

She shook her head, unable to speak, unable to deny it with words.

"Yes, you were," he murmured huskily.

She could feel the heat of his hands, attacking her defenses, trying to climb the barrier she'd fought hard to maintain.

She had to find her voice. "It wasn't a come-on."

"No, it was a turn-on." He began to nuzzle her neck.

Oh Lord.

She gave a shaky breath. "We're more than this, Matt."

He stopped nuzzling and leaned back, the look in his eyes pure passion. "Are we?"

It was honesty at its most basic.

He wanted her and she wanted him and that's what this was all about. It was what they'd been about the first time they'd made love, and nothing had changed between them on that front.

Did she really want to deny either of them the pleasure?

Worse, if she did, would he go find another warm body?

Would he walk out that door and leave her alone tonight? And then she would go to her bed and sleep alone and there would be no Matt to take her over the edge into fulfillment. No Matt to ease this profound hunger inside her. She didn't think her body could handle that right now. She was ripe for making love, no matter how much she wanted to refute that.

Her small purse slipped from her hand and fell to the carpet with a soft clink. "Oh God, I want you, Matt," she whispered, wrapping her arms around his neck.

His eyes flared with a triumph that normally would have her retracting her statement, yet this time it did nothing but thrill her.

She wanted him so badly.

He took her mouth in a fierce, hungry kiss and she parted her lips in full capitulation and kissed him back, rejoicing in his tongue slipping inside to devour her softness.

She moaned and he replied with a sound of satisfaction deep in his throat, his hands tightening on her waist as he pressed her up against the wall, leaving her with no illusion that he was fully aroused.

But his touch merely fueled the ache deep inside her, and she moaned again.

A deep, heartfelt moan.

She soon matched him stroke for stroke as a hypnotic blend of sensuality and seduction tantalized her senses.

His taste was heady.

He smelled…intoxicating.

He began showering kisses on her eyelids, down her cheek, along her chin, returning to her mouth time and time again, demanding a response she freely gave.

His hand closed possessively over her breast and a whimper escaped her throat as he explored the sensitive flesh through the material, teasing her, rubbing his thumb over her nipple. Could he feel the hammering of her heart? she wondered as a river of anticipation raced through her veins.

Soon it wasn't enough.

For either of them.

He swung her up in his arms and started down the hallway with her, twice stopping to kiss her boneless, turning her into a melting puddle of need by the time they reached his bedroom.

She registered a fleeting glimpse of the room decorated in olive and black before he was back to kissing her, carrying her over toward the bed, but not laying her down on it.

He stood her on her feet and in the catch of a breath, he unzipped her dress and pushed it down to the floor, along with her panties and silk stockings. Her shoes were somehow missing, so she must have already kicked them off along the way. He straightened and undid her lacy bra and tossed it aside.

Time came to an instant standstill.

She was naked.

Fully naked.

She realized he'd never seen her like this before.

His eyes drank her up and he made a guttural sound as he reached for her.

And time started ticking again.

They had to have each other.

Soon she tingled under his fingertips, making her ache in secret places that craved the heat of his arousal. Adrenaline pumped through her veins, her need shocking her.

Suddenly she couldn't wait a moment more to have Matt inside her. Giddily she pushed aside the flaps of his jacket and started to unbutton his shirt. Where his tie had gone she didn't know.

She must have been too slow because he groaned and stepped back, not to strip off his clothes as she thought, but to undo his trousers and free himself.

She gasped; then need kicked in and with her response matching his own urgency, she reached out to explore the hard lines of him.

"Stop," he growled as he reached down to the bedside drawer where he took out a condom.

She was about to say that she was on contraceptives to help with her monthly cycle, but she was suddenly…consciously…mesmerized by him rolling the condom on himself.

The words escaped her.

Then he was leaning her up against the bedroom

wall and maneuvering her body. She felt his erection at the tip of her entrance, felt him ease her onto him.

He slowly thrust upward and slid fully inside.

"Matt!" she cried out, gripping his shoulders, her eyes widening as her body adjusted to him.

A dark flush spread across his cheeks. "You feel so good."

"You, too," she gasped.

He lifted her and with a groan drove himself into her again, this time more firmly.

Their bodies locked and her senses spun.

She pressed a kiss against the hard cords in his neck. "Take me, Matt. Take me please."

"Where?" he muttered.

"Anywhere. As long as it's with you."

He began to thrust in and out, causing a pure and explosive pleasure within her. Before too long her body started to vibrate in ripples, radiating outward and pulling everything in its path back within her, including this man inside.

The center of her being became a whirlpool of sensation, flooding her with desire. She came with a rush as it sucked her into its incredible and mind-blowing depths.

A minisecond later, Matt followed her into the sensual vortex.

Seven

Matt shuddered to an awesome climax as Lana's body clenched around him, holding him tight, not letting go until she'd taken everything from him.

Finally he caught his breath and his head cleared—and he shuddered for a very different reason. This woman had her grip on him in more ways than one.

He gave her a hard kiss, withdrew from her to lay her down on the bed.

What the hell had he done? he asked himself as he strode from the room to the bathroom. He stood at the bathroom mirror. Making love to her just now had been so good. So bloody good he'd wanted her again almost immediately.

Dammit, he'd been caught in a snare of his own device.

And all because of that kiss in his office the other day.

And because of that wallet tonight.

And because in the car she'd caressed her mouth with her fingertips. Seeing her do that had sent him over the edge.

It hadn't helped that he hadn't been with a woman for weeks now. Nor had he ever had a more sensual relationship with a woman without actually having sex with her.

He wouldn't be caught out again.

She could hand in as many wallets as she liked and it still wouldn't matter. She could walk around in that sexy nightgown and he still wouldn't let her tempt him.

She could even parade naked in front of him.

He grimaced. Well, maybe not naked. He *was* a man, after all. He had his limits.

And he'd reached his limit tonight.

He would have to stop this right here.

He went back into the bedroom and stopped at the sight of her. Her short blond hair was tousled around her beautiful face, and she'd thrown her dress on but hadn't done up the zipper, the material falling away and leaving a smooth shoulder. In one hand she held her lacy bra and as she straightened with her panties in the other hand, he caught a glimpse of bare cheek.

Desire licked at his insides.

He swallowed hard. "I'm sorry, Lana, but this was a mistake."

She colored a little. "A...mistake?"

His lips formed a hard line. "I don't want you getting the wrong idea about this. It happened, but it's not going to happen again. It'll just get too complicated otherwise."

Something shifted in her expression. "Fine."

Her comment brought him up short.

He scowled. "It is?"

Her lips twisted. "Matt, you can forgive yourself for wanting someone you despise."

He felt a punch to his gut. "I don't despise you."

"Don't you? Funny, I thought you did."

"Lana, look—"

"Matt, really, I understand. We'd both had a few drinks tonight and—"

"One. That's all I had."

She blinked. "One?"

"I don't drink over the limit and drive."

She crinkled her nose. "Okay, so *I* had a couple of drinks and let down my guard. Seems to be my modus operandi. But at least we don't have to worry about a pregnancy this time."

The words jarred him. "That's something, I suppose."

Her chin angled with pride. "Now, if you'll excuse me, I'd like to go to my room and get some sleep. I need to get up early and go pick up Megan."

She was taking it so well.

Too well?

"We'll pick up Megan," he insisted as she passed him by.

She inclined her head and he let her go, one part of him amazed that for the first time he was letting a woman walk away from his bed while he still wanted more of her.

That's the way it had to be.

With Lana it was a necessity.

There was always a price to pay for happiness, Lana reminded herself as she sat on her bed and pressed her fingers to her temples.

And she'd just paid it.

Heavens, had she really made love with Matt again? Really melted at his touch? Had she really reached out and touched him like that?

Oh yeah.

It hadn't been quite as fast as the last time they'd made love in the office. Back then there had been no time for more than quick touches and furtive glances. No time for savoring each other. He'd thrust inside her before she'd known it and she'd welcomed him, joining him in a long, simultaneous climax. It had been the most incredible feeling she'd ever experienced.

Tonight had been just as incredible.

More so.

A mistake, he'd called it.

She winced. Yes, it had been a mistake. She'd reached that conclusion herself the moment he'd left her alone and sanity had returned. Oh, there'd been no doubt he'd wanted her and she'd wanted him and it had been enough at the time.

But now she had to wonder about the true reason behind it all. Had it merely been masculine pride? His friends had liked her and he'd said others would expect they'd have a physical relationship.

Or perhaps she'd been a convenience more than anything? She'd been unwittingly available when he'd wanted a woman.

Any woman.

Maybe her handing in the wallet had convinced him for a short time that she wasn't capable of stealing? And afterward reality had hit him with a thud and he was back to believing the worst of her again.

And now his guard was truly up.

Except the reality was that she hadn't expected anything more.

And he had no need to be on guard.

They'd merely been a man and woman in the wrong place at the right time. That's how she'd look at it. No need to get worked up about it all, right? She'd simply be grateful Matt wasn't feeling guilty and wanting to rectify the situation by insisting their marriage become permanent.

Thank God he hadn't.

Flinging aside her thoughts, she put on her nightgown, slid beneath the covers and turned off the light. And she'd try not to go over their lovemaking in minute detail. From now on she'd try and forget it ever happened.

Tomorrow they'd both move forward like mature adults.

Thankfully Lana was kept busy over the weekend. They both slept late in their separate beds, so that by the time they went to pick up Megan it was almost noon and Isabel insisted they stay for lunch.

Lana felt uncomfortable with Isabel's and Cesare's eyes on them, even guilty. If she and Matt had been on friendlier terms, she'd jokingly confess she felt like a teenager who'd had sex with her boyfriend and was trying not to let her parents know it.

As it was, they acted civil to each other until it was time to go home. She fully expected him to go out that evening, but to her surprise he went to the study. It was as if he was showing her he could be around her without making love to her again.

Or perhaps he was trying to show himself.

And that made her wonder, especially when she caught him watching her at odd times, his eyes darkening before he'd blank them out, as if a dial were turning on without his permission and he had to turn it off deliberately.

Unfortunately for her, she couldn't stop her thoughts from turning to their lovemaking. If only she could turn that part of her mind off, perhaps she could get some peace. If only Matt didn't affect her, she might have a chance at it. Truth to tell, she was dismayed at the way her body continued to want him again. It was as if there were still lively little sparks of desire floating in the air between them, in spite of her best efforts to put them out.

Her only consolation was that both of them were fighting this thing. She knew for sure that Matt wouldn't attempt to make love to her again.

And she wouldn't let him.

Thank heavens by midweek they were almost back to normal. Normal for them, that is.

Subsequently, when Matt walked into her office before lunch on Thursday she pretended she could ignore him.

"What are you doing?"

She glanced at him, then back to the computer screen. "Guess."

He expelled a breath. "Lana, I've checked those old accounts and there's nothing else there. If there was, I would have found it."

"No, there's something more. I can feel it. I—" She fell back in her chair as a thought made her heart skip a beat. "Are you saying you believe I didn't do it?"

His eyebrow slanted. "Let's say I'm giving you the slight benefit of the doubt."

"How kind," she drawled, pretending that even his halfhearted support didn't thrill her. It did. Perhaps he was getting to know the real her. He had to know she wasn't a person who would steal from others. Hadn't returning the wallet made him see that?

She mentally slumped. She shouldn't give too much credence to what he said. If he could make love to her while believing her a thief, then he could as easily change his mind about this.

"Come on. We're going out to lunch," he muttered.

Her mind whirled in surprise, then withdrew. "I'd rather stay here and look through these."

"I want to go shopping."

She sat up straight. "I told you I don't want any clothes."

"It's not for you. I'm going to buy some things for Megan's room."

"Things?"

"Furniture."

She lifted her chin. "I spent a lot of money on her furniture." She saw his eyes flicker. "Not stolen money," she said, feeling as if they were back where they started.

He inclined his head. "And you did well," he conceded, "but I want her to have the very best. Now that she's used to her new room, it's time for new furniture."

His words reminded her of a discussion at the ballet. "Didn't I hear your friend Justin talking about buying baby furniture for his son's room?"

He scowled. "Yeah, so?"

She tilted her head. "You don't have to one-up him, you know."

"I won't even bother to reply to that," he snapped, then looked at his watch. "I've made a booking and we're going to be late."

"Since when does that worry you?"

"It doesn't."

Sighing, she grabbed her purse and stood up. "I've already had a piece of cake for morning tea."

"Your figure can handle lunch."

The compliment sent the blood rushing to her head, but she concentrated on getting out of the room. He took her elbow as she passed him by, bringing her close but not too close as he walked her from the room and down the corridor. She wasn't sure if his hold was to remind everyone she was his wife, or to let *her* know who was boss.

Probably both, she mused, knowing in either case it was a proprietary gesture and nothing more.

Ten minutes later they were seated at a restaurant with a glorious view of the Royal Botanic Gardens. The weather was perfect for a lunchtime walk or a jog, and many people were doing exactly that along the pathways. Others were sitting on the grass and taking in the harbor view.

Lana wished she was sitting out there in the sunshine, rather than sitting in here with Matt. Out there she could escape being close to him. In here there was no escape.

"We need to talk," Matt said, once they'd ordered a light lunch. "About Megan."

Her heart seemed to squeeze tight. Did he want

a divorce already? No, then he wouldn't want to furnish Megan's room.

A wave of apprehension swept through her as her old fear rose. Perhaps he wanted Megan, but wanted to get rid of *her?* Perhaps he'd found a way to push her out of her daughter's life?

He leaned back in his chair. "I've located a new day care center for her."

Lana's shoulders slumped. "Is that all?"

He scowled. "What did you think I wanted to talk about?"

"I thought you were going to finally offer to buy Megan off me."

His eyes narrowed. "Would you sell her?"

She looked him straight in the eye. "I'd rather die first."

Silence; then he said with a twitch of his lips, "Defeats the purpose, don't you think?"

"You know what I mean."

His humor disappeared. "I wouldn't ask that of you, Lana. I can see you love Megan more than life itself."

A warm feeling bounced inside her chest. "Thank you."

Their gazes linked, and all at once Lana felt they connected on a level beyond the bedroom. For a moment they both saw a true part of each other, not the facade they sought to present.

Then the waiter provided a diversion by returning with their drinks, and she broke eye contact and took a sip of her mineral water to give herself something to do.

"Now, back to the day care center," Matt said brusquely once they were alone. "I've found a suitable one not too far away."

Suddenly Lana felt apprehensive. "You have?"

His eyes narrowed. "What's the matter? I thought you'd be happy."

"I am. I mean, I am, but I'm not."

"That makes sense," he drawled.

She grimaced. "I'm frightened for her safety, Matt. I didn't have to worry about that before, but now it's a real threat."

He considered that. "I'll make sure she's safe, Lana."

She let out a slow breath of relief. "I know you will."

He held her gaze, a pleased look in his eyes. "Have you considered that she may not need to go to day care at all? She's only little. It might be best for her to continue staying at home with Ruth on the days that you're working. What do you think?"

That thought had occurred to her, too, but she shook her head. "No. She needs to get used to it again. Next year there'll be just me and her and…"

"You don't have to worry about any of that," he said, his face closed now.

She paused a moment. Then said, "You know, Matt, I don't say no just to be difficult. I do whatever's good for Megan, despite what's good for us."

He held himself stiffly. "I appreciate that."

Suddenly she felt sorry for him. His whole life had changed. "But I have to admit it's been a new experience for me, sharing responsibility for her like this," she conceded. "It takes time to get used to it."

A friendlier look entered her eyes. "She's *our* responsibility, Lana. Don't forget that."

His words sent a quiver of delight through her veins. He wasn't being possessive of Megan, or arrogant toward *her*. He was merely acknowledging their mutual love for the most important person in their lives.

As it should be.

Lunch arrived, and Lana fought back disappointment at the interruption. She and Matt had bonded a moment ago and she liked the feeling.

If only…

What?

If only Matt could really believe she wasn't the bad person he thought she was?

If only he didn't need proof she hadn't stolen the money?

If only they could end up friends for Megan's sake?

She sighed, knowing that wasn't possible. There was too much between them now for them ever to be friends.

They finished eating in silence, then had coffee. She drank hers down quickly, wanting to get this over and done with and get back to work. The less time spent in Matt's company the better. She was getting too soft where he was concerned.

Matt took a last mouthful of coffee. "Right. Let's go shopping."

He drove them to a baby boutique that she remembered Justin mentioning. She shot him a wry look as they got out of the car.

"He recommended it, that's all," he defended, but she saw the humorous gleam in those dark eyes, and a soft glow filled her.

The manager came out to greet them the minute they stepped inside the store. "Mr. and Mrs. Valente," he welcomed, and Lana shot Matt another knowing look, which he ignored this time.

The store manager knew a good sale coming and he was extremely helpful. As for Matt, he was businesslike on the outside, but she could see he was enjoying himself. He ordered a new crib, then saw something better that would turn into a bed for Megan's future use, and ordered that one instead. He did the same with a toy box and a stroller. And he wanted to buy the biggest playpen there.

Lana saw the playpen and laughed.

"What's so funny?" he asked as the store manager went off to see about delivery.

"You. You're like a kid in a toy store."

He shrugged. "Hey, it's not every day a man gets to buy things for his daughter. Besides, we *are* in a toy store."

"Enjoy it while you can. I doubt she'll let you when she gets older."

They shared a smile that could have deepened to something more, only her cell phone rang. It was Ruth saying Megan had a high temperature and wasn't well.

"We'll be right there," she said, seeing Matt pull his shoulders back as if expecting a blow.

"Megan?" he muttered after she'd ended her call.

Lana nodded, worry already eating at her. "She's got a temperature."

Matt put his arm under her elbow, speaking to the store manager as he guided her to the front door. "Our daughter's sick. I'll get my PA to call you and arrange payment."

"Very good, sir. I hope your daughter is okay."

"So do I," Matt said, his voice as rough as gravel.

Lana's heart was in her mouth as they drove home. "She might be teething, Matt. That's probably all it is."

"Teething doesn't make them sick."

She glanced sideways at him. "How do you know that?"

"I've read some books about it."

That surprised her. "A lot of doctors say that teething doesn't make them sick, but I've heard it lowers a child's resistance to picking up germs."

"Germs?" he asked, as if she'd said a dirty word.

"Cold germs, that's all." She could see the grimness on Matt's face and she felt sorry for him. The playboy was truly gone right now, and in its place was a very worried father.

"Do you have a family doctor?" he asked.

"Not really."

His mouth tightened as he used his cell phone to call his mother, telling her the situation and shooting out instructions.

He hung up. "Mum will get our family doctor to pay a visit."

"Good," Lana murmured.

She usually visited the local medical center if she or Megan needed a doctor, though she wasn't sure Matt could understand that. He had wealth and connections, and for the first time ever, she thanked God he did. She wanted the best for her daughter.

As soon as Ruth opened the door, Megan cried out to Lana, who hurried forward and took her daughter in her arms. Lana's heart lurched at Megan's rosy red cheeks, stained by tears. She wore only a diaper and felt hot to the touch.

Then Megan saw Matt, gave a loud cry and threw her arms out toward him, wanting to be held by her father. Lana looked at Matt and her legs almost gave out at the sheer love for his daughter on his face. She willingly handed Megan over to him.

"I've given her some medicine," Ruth said calmly as they moved inside. "And I've been cooling her down in the bath."

"Thank you, Ruth," Lana said, looking at her daughter with a worried frown. "Let's take her into the living room, Matt."

"I'll just go wet this washcloth again for her," Ruth said.

Once in the living room, Megan whimpered and Matt looked helpless all of a sudden. "Shouldn't we take her to the hospital?"

Lana tried not to show her worry. "Let's give the medication a chance to work until the doctor gets here."

Megan started crying again and he tried to soothe her. "Dammit, where is that bloody doctor?"

Lana wiped her daughter's nose with a tissue. "Try not to worry, Matt. Kids can look so sick one minute and the next they're up and running around." She gave a sympathetic smile. "Believe me, there were some nights I walked the floor with her when she had a cold or colic and I would have sworn she had pneumonia or something worse."

Matt stiffened. "I would have been there if I'd known."

She groaned inwardly. "It wasn't a criticism of you."

Megan continued crying and he shot Lana a dark look. "Really? It sounded like it to me."

She knew he was panicking deep inside, so she allowed him his snide remark. "Matt, I was only trying to say she'll be back to normal in no time. Just take it easy."

"Like you're doing?" he snapped, as Megan continued crying. "You seem to be taking this real easy. But you're an old hand at this, aren't you?"

She angled her chin. "That's enough, Matt."

"No, it's—"

"Mr. Valente," Ruth warned, coming back into the room with the washcloth. "This is not the time or place to be arguing. Your daughter is sick. She needs you to remain calm." She sounded like a schoolteacher reprimanding one of her students, and Matt's face blanched.

A moment crept by.

He let out a slow breath. "You're right, Ruth." He looked at Lana. "I'm sorry, Lana. I didn't mean to snap at you."

"I know, Matt."

After that the doctor came and said it was probably only a virus but to keep an eye on her. The medication had worked by then, so the little girl soon fell asleep.

They continued to anxiously check on her throughout the evening, unable to sit still for long. By midnight she woke and was cool to the touch, and they each breathed a sigh of relief. It appeared the worst was over. After a drink of water, she fell asleep again.

"Lana, I'm really sorry about snapping at you today," Matt murmured, standing by the crib.

She realized she had finally given himself permission to relax now that Megan was on the mend. "Matt, I understand. You were scared something serious was the matter with her."

His mouth flattened into a grim line. "It doesn't excuse me taking it out on you. Hell, I can only imagine how it must feel to be alone and carrying the full weight of it all."

"Don't beat yourself up about it."

He stood still for a moment longer, looking down at his sleeping daughter. Then he looked up. "Why don't you go to bed," he suggested quietly. "You should get some sleep."

"But you're the one with work tomorrow." She at least had a day off.

"I don't have to go in if she's not better." Then he heaved a sigh. "I suppose we should both go to bed," he said, nothing remotely suggestive in his words.

Lana nodded. "It's been a long day."

He went to move away, then stopped. "Call me if I don't hear her."

"I will."

He left the room and exhaustion swooped over Lana. The thought of bed and sleep sounded like heaven.

Only, once she'd had her shower she felt incredibly thirsty and decided to get a cool glass of milk or she wouldn't sleep until she did.

And this time she remembered to slip on her satiny bathrobe over her chemise nightgown.

Just in case.

It was as well she did. At the kitchen door she got a jolt to find Matt standing there in his pajama bottoms, looking out the window over the back garden, the moon giving enough light for her to see his knuckles gripping the edge of the sink.

She moved toward him in concern. "Matt?"

He didn't turn around.

"Matt, are you okay?"

He took a ragged breath. "I'm not sure I can handle this parenting stuff, Lana," he muttered. "Tonight almost killed me worrying about her."

Her heart softened. Oh, she so knew how he felt. It was a tough job at times.

"Too late," she said gently. "Once you're a parent there's no going back. She has our heart." Without thinking, she rested her hand on his shoulder and felt his muscles tighten.

"Don't touch me, Lana. Not right now. Not tonight."

The breath hitched in her throat. "Why?"

"I may not be responsible for my actions."

A knot rose in her throat. "Then don't be," she whispered, squeezing his shoulder.

He sucked in a sharp breath and slowly turned to face her, his eyes riveting on her face. "Are you sure?"

She nodded.

His hands slid onto her hips and held. "I've never wanted a woman like I want you."

Oh God, he was turning her into mush.

"If we make love, I'm going to share your bed from now on, Lana."

She swallowed. "You are?"

"It's no use us pretending we don't want each other."

Her heart thudded. Did he mean…

"But I make no promises."

Her heart hit the floor, then picked itself up.

Her eyes clung to his. "I don't want any promises, Matt. I don't want anything but for you to make love to me over and over."

He groaned and pulled her into his arms, his mouth capturing hers, her lips opening in invitation. He took slow sips from her mouth, drugging her with his taste and his velvety tongue.

And then he stepped back and held out his hand, his eyes glittering in the dark. "Shall we make ourselves more comfortable?"

Without hesitation she slipped her hand in his, happy to follow him wherever he led.

They stopped briefly to check on their daughter, who thankfully continued to sleep peacefully, and they smiled at each other with deep connection.

Then they went into his room and shut the door behind them, tucking themselves away, fully aware there was no need to hurry their lovemaking this time.

He held her in front of him. "You're gorgeous," he said huskily, his eyes going over her from the top of her head, down over her satiny bathrobe, to her bare feet. Then his eyes rose upward. "God. I almost don't want to take your clothes off you."

She became fascinated by the vein that pulsed in his neck. "You don't?"

"I'm lying."

She moistened her lips. "I'm glad."

"So am I," he murmured, undoing the sash at her

waist and peeling the robe off her shoulders, leaving her standing there in her pearl-colored chemise. "Oh yeah, sweetheart. I'm…so…glad."

He pulled her close and started kissing her again. Deeply, this time.

Deeper than any other time, not so much in touch but in intensity.

And intimacy.

This time it wasn't about two people making love together, but about two people being intimate.

And then he reached down to her hem and lifted the nightgown over her head, leaving her naked.

She gasped as his hands slow-traced her hips… her derriere…brushing over the bare skin of her back…exploring her body from behind.

And then those wonderful hands moved up and around to her front, touching her breasts, circling the sensitive skin before cupping them as he weighed and measured them in his palms, before lowering his head and fitting one of the brown nubs in his mouth.

"Oh my heaven," was all she could manage, her mind reeling as he gently nipped and licked her body to life…a life that had her clutching his bare shoulders, wanting to touch him as he was touching her.

She was almost ready to sink to the floor by the time he moved back, but she somehow managed to speak. "Please, Matt. My turn."

A light smoldered in his eyes. "Go ahead."

A flash of heat washed over her and suddenly her hands shook, but that didn't stop her from sliding her palms over his hair-roughened chest, reveling in the hot feel of him beneath her palms.

He shuddered and her head spun and she grew more daring, her hands sliding down over the tight muscles of his stomach, over the front of his pajama pants to where he felt hard and demanding.

"Stop," he rasped.

She stood her ground. "No." She pushed his pants down until they reached his feet.

Swearing softly, he stepped out of them and kicked them aside and she made her way up his naked flesh, running her hands up along his flanks, across to his powerful erection, where she fondled him, loving the sound of his groan and the shudder of his body before she stood back to fully admire him for the first time ever.

He was fully exposed.

There was nothing left but *him*.

The utterly perfect male.

She reached for him again, but he put his hand over hers. "No." His gaze dropped down to her thighs, then shot back up. "Do you realize I've never tasted you? Not once."

His words sent electrifying shivers down her spine. "Then don't let me stop you."

Growling satisfaction, he dropped to his knees.

Her legs shook as he began kissing her in a more intimate way. She was acutely aware of his dark head at the junction of her thighs, doing marvelous things to her, his tongue warm and smooth, enticingly so.

She trembled, verging on the edge of discovery. She was almost ready to topple.

"Not yet," he muttered, and the next thing she knew he was lowering her onto the bed, her body still one big ache, craving that joyous feeling just out of reach.

He opened the bedside drawer and took out a foil packet, and instantly her mind cleared even as her body still hungered for release.

"Matt, stop."

He paused, looking at her with a question in his eyes.

"You don't need those."

"I don't?"

"I'm protected." She saw him wince and the past came back to haunt her. At the Christmas party it had been over before they knew it, and afterward she'd lied about protection so he wouldn't worry about her becoming pregnant. "I'm telling the truth this time, Matt."

She held his gaze.

If he didn't believe her she couldn't proceed.

He stared hard for a couple of loaded seconds, then dropped the foil back in the drawer. The mattress lurched as he joined her, just as her heart was lurching in her chest. He stretched out on top of her, his arms pure steel, holding him up to look down at her from above.

His eyes trapped hers for a heart-stopping moment.

And he grew rigid between her legs.

"Thank you for trusting me," she said sincerely.

"No, thank *you* for giving me our daughter."

Her vision blurred as tender warmth entered her heart. Then she took a ragged breath. "I'm yours tonight, Matt," she murmured, and let her thighs fall open so that he could find his way.

He entered her and she moved to meet him. Soon after, she cried out his name, delicious contractions hitting her until she abandoned herself to a spine-tingling fusion to become one with him.

One body.

One heartbeat.

Her one true love.

"Are you okay?"

Lana heard the words in her ear but couldn't reply. How had it happened? How had she tumbled headlong into love with him? She was staggered by the revelation.

Oh Lord.

He stayed inside her and looked down into her eyes. "Lana?"

She thought fast.

"Just catching my breath," she said with a smile, her fingers itching to run lovingly along his jaw.

She daren't.

He studied her without giving anything away himself. "No regrets?"

Could she regret that she loved him?

She shook her head. "Not this time."

His face relaxed. "Me either." Leaning down, he gave her a long, soft kiss that made her want to stay in his arms for the rest of her life.

Eventually he lifted his head. "I've never made love to any other woman without a condom."

"I know. You told me that the first time we made love."

"I remember." His eyes darkened. "And you believed me."

"Of course," she said without hesitation.

His gaze searched her eyes. Then slid down to where the tips of her breasts pressed against his chest. "I want you again."

Her eyes widened as she felt him grow hard inside her. "So soon?"

"Yes."

She swallowed. He was looking at her as if he wanted her more than anything else in the world. The feeling was so new it made her blush.

"Don't you need to gather your strength?" she babbled, suddenly self-conscious that a man wanted her so much.

And not just any man.

Matt.

"I'm stronger than I look," he muttered.

She acknowledged something when she heard those words.

He *was* strong.

In every way.

And it wasn't just physical either. She'd known

men who were muscular but hollow. Others had been too strong for their own good and would never let a woman see their softer side as Matt had this evening over Megan.

But Matt, oh yes, he just seemed to fit her like a piece in a jigsaw puzzle. Everything he did, everything he was, seemed tailor-made for her.

It gave her a sense of rightness as Matt began to make love to her all over again. And afterward, when she rested her cheek drowsily on his chest, two thoughts crossed her mind before she fell into an exhausted slumber.

Yes, she loved this man.

But sometimes love wasn't enough.

Eight

Matt ignored the budget reports waiting on his desk and sat back in his chair for a moment. He was still reeling from seeing Megan sick yesterday. Thank God she was better now.

Lord, when she'd held out her little arms to him he thought his heart would explode with love and concern. He was learning that loving a child was a bittersweet pain. Lana was right. Once you saw your child and the love entered your heart, there was no going back.

Lana was an old hand at this now. She'd done this by herself for the last eleven months. Not to mention coping with being pregnant.

Something turned over in his chest at the thought

of her carrying his baby. To have been pregnant and alone with only an uncle a world away in France must have been terrifying.

He felt humble.

And could he really blame her now if she'd stolen that money to support her and her child?

If?

Yes, he had his doubts now and with each day they were growing stronger. But hell, he was still angry deep inside that she hadn't come to him about her pregnancy. He really didn't understand why she hadn't.

Yet she'd supported him yesterday over Megan and then again late in the night when she'd offered herself to him. If she didn't have some sort of feelings for him, would she have done either of those things?

Of course having *some* feelings was like having *some* money. A person could get by on a small amount, but it wasn't enough to build a house.

Or a marriage.

That's if a person wanted to build a house in the first place, which neither he nor Lana wanted. They were both only looking to put a roof over their daughter's head.

Dammit, Lana had come into his life with the greatest gift in her arms.

And he was now going to share her bed full-time until their divorce.

And *still* he couldn't figure her out.

Perhaps he shouldn't even try, he decided, accepting that some things were a mystery.

Just then the intercom buzzed.

"Matt, there's a gentleman on the line from France looking for Lana," Irene said. "He said he's her uncle."

Matt frowned. "Put him through, Irene." He waited a moment for the connection to go through. "Matt Valente here."

"Matt? I'm pleased to meet you. It's Dan Moore here. Lana's uncle. I've just got back from a trip to South Africa and I read the letter from Lana about her marriage. Congratulations. Lana's a wonderful girl."

"Thank you, Dan. Yes, she is."

"I'm sorry I missed the wedding. I would have been there if I'd known, but I understand the rush for little Megan's sake."

So he knew the reason for the marriage.

"Yes."

"I don't have your home number but if you could get Lana to give me a call that would be terrific. I need to tell her that now she's married to you, I want to deed the apartment over to Megan."

Matt's heart thudded. "The apartment?"

"Yes. Lana would have told you I bought it for her and Megan."

"Of course," he lied without missing a beat.

So *that's* where the money had come from.

"I want it to be my gift to my great-niece. I don't

ever want her to be alone like Lana was when her parents died." He took a breath. "Not that they were much use to her when they were living, God rest their souls. She would have told you about that, too, no doubt." He paused. "Unfortunately I was living in France and couldn't be there for her, but she always knew I was just a phone call away."

Matt felt a band of tightness in his chest. He should have read that report his father had ordered on Lana and her family. It would have explained a lot about the pieces that made up his wife.

"I won't let that happen to Megan, Dan. She will always have me and my family to look after her."

For all that, he suddenly realized he didn't like the thought of sharing his daughter with some unknown person. Not even one of Lana's relatives.

"That's good to know, Matt. Please give Lana my love and tell her Aimee and Julien send their love, too. I'll talk to her soon."

Matt was curious. "Is Julien your son?"

There was a moment's hesitation. "So Lana hasn't told you yet? I guess it's not an easy thing for her to say, but I'd appreciate if you could keep this in the family."

"Tell me what?"

"Julien is my lover."

Lana spent the day trying to come to terms with loving Matt, knowing she could never tell him.

If it had been only her and Matt, then she might

have given it a shot. She was strong enough to walk away if things turned bad.

She couldn't take such a chance when she had a responsibility to her daughter. Matt was great with Megan, but she couldn't stand back and let Matt's disdain for *her* become a part of their lives.

She wouldn't.

When Matt arrived home later that day, she hid her love from him and prayed to God she could keep doing it until the year was up. Their physical relationship would have to be enough.

So why hadn't he kissed her hello?

And why didn't he pull her into his arms and hold her close? she wondered throughout dinner. Was this the way it was going to be? Were they just going to be lovers in the bedroom and nothing else?

Her heart slumped against her rib cage as she realized something. He hadn't asked Ruth to move his things into the master bedroom. Or was he going to do it himself? Were they even going to share a bed now?

Oh God.

Was Matt having second thoughts?

She was tempted to come right out and ask him, once they'd put Megan to bed and were sitting in the living room watching television. At least they could talk without any interruption, Ruth having left a short while ago to spend the night at her sister's place.

She was working up the courage to speak when

without warning he grabbed the remote and turned the television off.

"I had a phone call today," he said. "From Dan Moore."

Her eyes went wide. "Uncle Dan?"

He nodded. "He received your letter but he didn't know the phone number for the house, so he called you at work. Irene put him through to me."

"And?"

"He'd just gotten back from South Africa. He wanted you to know he was delighted about your marriage and he sent his love." He watched her carefully. "He also said to tell you that Aimee and Julien send their love."

She blinked, then quickly pretended to brush some lint off her dress. "How nice."

Silence.

"Why didn't you tell me, Lana?"

She looked up. "What?"

"That your uncle is bisexual."

She gave a soft gasp. "How do you know that?"

"Dan told me Julien was his lover." He grimaced. "Did you expect me to be shocked? His sexual preferences don't matter to me."

"They do to the press. I owe Dan so much. I'd hate to repay him by having his private life dragged out in the open."

"I wouldn't tell the press. They'd be the last I'd tell anything."

She shook her head. "Matt, just being related to

a Valente is enough to send them into a media feeding frenzy. We were lucky that they romanticized our wedding because of Megan, but Dan's reputation wouldn't escape so easily."

He studied her. "He's the reason you let me believe you'd bought the apartment with the stolen money?"

Her eyes widened. "You know about that too?"

"Dan said he wanted to deed the apartment he bought you over to Megan."

"Oh, he's such a lovely man." Then she remembered something. "I'm surprised you didn't find all this when you did a background check on me. And I know you would have done one, Matt. I'm not naïve. It's a necessary evil for people with money."

"My father ordered the report on you. I didn't read it, but he gave me a brief rundown and that was all." He frowned. "I should have read it. It might have saved a lot of arguments between us."

"But it might not have said anything about Dan and Julien. I was just fearful in case that did come to light and someone somewhere leaked it to the papers."

He considered her for a long moment.

"Tell me about your parents, Lana."

She started in surprise, then groaned inwardly. If Matt had loved her she would have no hesitation in telling him about her background. People in love did that sort of thing, sharing their deepest thoughts and feelings.

But there was only one of them in love here.

Her.

Then she looked at him and saw a determined look in his eyes that said he wouldn't let her hold back.

"My parents' marriage was…abusive to say the least," she began, her throat croaky with words that had never been said before. "My father used to drink and he'd hit my mother, and my mother used to blame him for all her ills, and that in turn gave my father reason to drink. It was a vicious circle and I was caught in the middle." She drew a calming breath. "Thankfully Dan paid for me to go to boarding school when I turned twelve. Things were much better for me then."

A muscle knotted in his jaw. "I'm sorry."

She gave a strained smile. "Thank you, but there's no need."

Dear God, she hated thinking about those days. As a little girl her father had been remote and her mother had been loving and caring, but as the years passed it seemed that her mother had forgotten she had a daughter and had been hell-bent on making her husband's life a misery. Dan had tried to get his sister and brother-in-law some help, but they hadn't wanted it.

"From police reports they'd been arguing hours before the family home had burned to the ground with them in it."

"Bloody hell! I know they were dead but not how it happened."

"I know. It gives me nightmares sometimes."

There was a lengthy pause.

"Then I'm here to hold you." He held her eyes captive. "Come to me, Lana."

"Wh…what? There?" she said, looking at where he patted his lap. She was suddenly aware that they were alone.

"Yes, right here."

He waited.

She got to her feet and closed the gap between them, sinking down to sit on his lap. It felt strange sitting here like this with him.

"Look at me."

She lifted her head to look him in the eye.

He ran his palm up and down her shoulder in a comforting gesture. "I don't want you to feel alone anymore, Lana."

"I don't. I have Megan."

"You have me, too. Even after all this is over, I'll still be here for you."

Her heart rolled over. He didn't love her but he was showing her he cared about her. Oh, how she wished things could be different.

"Thank you, Matt," she said huskily.

He put his fingers under her chin. "Come here."

She frowned. "What do you mean?"

"Closer," he murmured, tugging her chin toward him. "I want your lips against mine. I want my body against yours. I want to be inside you."

Oh my.

"Yes." She wanted that, too.

Very much.

He cupped her face and silenced her with a kiss, and she realized that sex was his way of showing her comfort. Her heart swelled with the depth of her feelings for him.

He turned off the lamps, leaving the room bathed in shimmering light from the swimming pool outside. It gave a dreamlike quality to their togetherness as he lowered her to the thick living room rug and made slow, tender love to her.

It was so exquisite…so sweet…she cried afterward and he held her close. She'd never allowed another adult such free range of her heart before.

It stunned her.

He was truly a part of her now.

And no matter what happened in the future, no one could take this away from her.

Nine

Lana proceeded with caution over the next two weeks, her marriage to Matt having now deepened into a firm personal relationship. Yet she had to keep reminding herself it was only temporary.

And she fought herself constantly not to let him know that she loved him, especially when they made love every night, then slept, entwined together. It was wonderful waking up in his arms.

They watched television together after Megan went to bed, or they sat reading books, or sometimes Matt worked beside her in the living room rather than in his study. And they spent as much time as they could with their daughter.

As a family.

A temporary one, she needed to keep telling herself.

And Matt actually spent time with her checking over the accounts, and that meant more to her than anything. It signified that he fully believed she had nothing to do with the stolen money and had been set up to take the fall if something was discovered.

And if that were the case, *who* had used her in such a fashion? She still suspected Evan. The man seemed to be in her office more often than not on some pretext or other. Once she'd even found him at her desk looking through some paperwork. She'd challenged him, but he'd said he was looking for a report.

In any case, it made her burn to catch the real perpetrator, whether that was Evan or not. That person had put her very reputation on the line. He shouldn't be allowed to get away with it.

The night before Megan's first birthday, Lana got up from the sofa and went over to the sideboard.

"Matt, I have something for you," she said, coming back with a photograph album in her hands. "I thought you might like to see some pictures of our daughter's life so far."

Something emotional crossed his face.

"You've never asked about her birth, but I thought you might like to know anyway," she said, sliding onto the sofa next to him.

He swallowed hard. "I didn't ask before because it was too painful."

"I figured that." She handed him the album.

He looked down, almost in slow motion, and opened the heavy cover, staring at the first item. It was a commemorative birth certificate with his name as the father.

He darted her a look, turned the page. A picture of Megan just a few hours old stared up at them. She was still wrinkly and her eyes were shut.

"She was beautiful," he said huskily.

She smiled. "Every parent thinks their child is beautiful."

He arched a brow. "You think I'm biased?"

"Definitely," she teased.

He picked up her hand and brought it to his lips. "Then she takes after her mother."

She caught her breath. "No, she's like you."

His lips twitched. "Are you saying I'm gorgeous?"

He was.

She flushed and drew his attention back to the album. If she told him the truth, would she give herself away? Would he see that she loved him?

"Look at that mop of black hair on her," he said, interrupting her thoughts.

"She's a Valente. What do you expect?"

He grinned, then continued to turn the pages until he came to the one of Lana. He frowned. "You were crying?"

"They call it the baby blues." She didn't say but she'd been upset because Matt hadn't been able to share in the joy of Megan's birth.

He held her eyes a minute, then returned to the album. Page after page they went through together. At the end he closed the book carefully and went to hand it to her.

She pushed it back to him. "It's for you to keep."

He seemed to hold himself in check. "Thank you."

She cleared her throat. She couldn't tell him she loved him, but there was something else that very much needed to be said.

"I'm sorry, Matt."

"Sorry?"

"For keeping her from you. If I'd known how much you would love her—" She broke off, unable to finish the words.

He tenderly ran a finger down her cheek, turning her heart over. "That means more to me than you know."

"It does?"

He nodded.

"I'm glad you're here for her first birthday, Matt."

"Me, too." He leaned toward her and kissed her softly on the lips. Then without warning, he got up with the album in his hands and walked out of the room.

Lana's throat closed up. She'd wanted him to take her in his arms and make love to her, even as she understood why he hadn't. He needed to be alone right now.

If only she could feel less alone herself.

* * *

Lana was excited about Megan's party but tried not to let it get the better of her. She recollected only too well the last party her own parents had given her on her tenth birthday. Her father had come home drunk and caused a scene in front of her friends. And her childhood humiliation had been complete.

Oh, she knew no one would cause a scene at Megan's party the way her own father had done years ago. That wasn't the Valentes' style, and thank the Lord it wasn't. She wouldn't be here if it was.

But she didn't want to get too emotionally attached to this family when in years to come, possibly even Megan's next birthday, she would not be invited along. It would only end in heartache for herself, despite Megan's emotional attachment to them being a positive thing for her daughter.

"Lana, smile," Sasha said, holding up the camera.

Her sister-in-law took a picture of her and Matt crouching down to help Megan unwrap one of the myriads of presents on the living room floor.

And suddenly Lana was a part of them.

They were all just so thrilled to have Megan in the family that she couldn't be aloof. She tried…God knows she tried…but their joy was catching.

She smiled, then quickly looked down at her daughter's head, her eyes misting over, but not before she caught a gentle look in Matt's eyes. He knew how much this meant to her.

They continued opening the presents. Olivia and

Alex's son, Scott, was disgusted that no one had bought Megan any boy-type gifts, but their six-year-old daughter, Renee, thought the doll was great.

"It's bigger than Megan is," Nick scoffed when he saw what Cesare and Isabel had given her.

Cesare puffed up with full confidence. "It won't be long before she grows big enough to play with it."

They moved into the dining room, where the party carried on. Matt had decorated it with balloons and streamers and Ruth had made a selection of party foods for everyone. There was a birthday cake shaped like a teddy bear and they all sang "Happy Birthday" while Megan sat at the head of the table in her high chair.

For a moment Lana thought Megan might cry, but Matt waved a streamer in front of her face and that caught the little girl's attention.

The song finished and Isabel leaned toward Lana. "Doesn't she look cute?"

A soft curve touched Lana's lips. "Yes, she—"

"Da-Da."

Lana blinked. Had she just heard right?

"Da-Da."

There was a moment's silence.

"Did she just say Da-Da?" Alex asked.

Lana looked at Matt, who seemed to be rooted to the floor. She'd heard, but had Matt?

"Yeah, she did," Nick said. "Matt, did—"

"Oh my God," Matt muttered, "she called me Da-Da." A look of pride burst in his eyes, turning

Lana's heart over with love. Suddenly he whooped with joy and spun toward her. "Lana, did you hear her? She called me Da-Da."

Without warning, Lana was pulled into his arms. He kissed her hard and quick, before he eased away, their gazes locking and sharing the moment.

She blinked back tears of joy. "Yes, I heard her, Matt," she said huskily.

Matt kissed her again, then let her go and turned to Megan, scooping her out of her high chair. "Come on, you little darling. Come to Da-Da."

Lana watched the two of them together. Matt unashamedly kissed his daughter's cheek, then hugged her tight, and Lana's love for him…for them both… filled her until she thought she might die with the depth of it.

Everyone started to laugh and joke, but she couldn't have smiled to save her life.

The moment was too emotional.

And then she became conscious of Cesare watching her from across the room, the intensity in his eyes telling her he realized she loved his son.

She looked away. She couldn't admit it to the older man, not even in a look. Her love for Matt was something she never wanted anyone to know.

As if drawn by a magnet, her eyes found their way back to her father-in-law. She couldn't help herself. He inclined his head, telling her in his own way that he was pleased about it.

Her throat closed up and she turned and left

quietly to go to the living room, needing time to gather herself together. She didn't want anyone else reading her mind.

Or her emotions.

It was bad enough that Cesare had.

Okay, take a deep breath. It was her emotions she had to get under control right now. This was her daughter's first birthday. She needed to concentrate on that.

It would be the first of many, she prayed.

Many *happy* birthdays.

She would make sure of that. Her daughter would know only love and happiness from her parents.

Unlike her own childhood.

And when Megan was old enough, Lana knew she would make sure her daughter didn't feel any blame over her parents' marriage. To give Megan the Valente name may have been the reason for her and Matt's marriage, but only because they loved her enough to put her first, not because it was expected of them.

"Lana?"

The hint of Italian accent told her Cesare had followed her.

She planted a smile on her face and turned to face him. "Cesare, what are you doing here? You should be back there with your family."

"They're your family, too, Lana."

She said nothing. She wanted to believe that, but they both knew she was only here because of Megan.

"You love my son."

She gasped, then looked behind him in case anyone else had followed and heard. Luckily they hadn't.

"I don't know where you'd get that idea."

"I saw the love in your eyes, Lana."

She winced inwardly. "For Megan's sake, that's all. I'm thrilled Matt loves her so much. He's a wonderful father."

"Naturally," Cesare said, inclining his head in the Valente manner. "But it's more than that. I've been married three times, *cara*. I know that look of love in a woman."

She tried to act nonchalant. "You're wrong, Cesare."

"I'm never wrong."

"Cesare, look, even if it were true, don't get your hopes up. Matt will never fall in love with me. He doesn't want to fall in love with any woman. He likes his freedom too much."

Cesare held her gaze. "You've asked him that, have you?"

"He told me that before we were married."

"He didn't know you then. Now he does."

That was true. Matt had believed her a thief at first, but now he didn't.

Hope rose inside her for a moment.

Then died.

"Cesare, it isn't a matter of knowing me. It's a matter of Matt knowing himself. He's a playboy.

There's simply no possibility he would want to make this a permanent arrangement."

"Lana—"

"Cesare, please don't look for something on his part that's not there."

He drew himself up. "I don't need to look further than my *naso*." He tapped his nose. "But perhaps you do, *cara*," he said pointedly, then turned and left the room.

Lana released a slow breath. Cesare was a good man. He loved his wife and family and would always be there for them. Unlike her own father…

And then she realized something.

Matt was like his father.

He was a good man, too.

He wasn't in the least like her own father. Up until now, deep down she'd been judging Matt by her father's standards. And that was wrong. Matt was a far, far better man than her father had ever been.

Renewed hope filled Lana.

Hope that she and Matt would never be like her parents.

Hope that she and Matt might actually be able to make a go of their marriage.

And perhaps he might even come to love her one day?

Her heart fluttered and a feeling of warmth stayed with her for the rest of the evening. She couldn't shake it. She didn't *want* to shake it. The look in Cesare's eyes had given her hope for a future with Matt.

"Megan had a great time, didn't she?" Matt murmured, coming up behind her as she stood looking over the crib once the party was over.

She nodded. "Everyone did by the looks of them."

"Did *you*?"

She smiled softly at him. "Oh yes."

"But you didn't expect to, did you, Lana?" He didn't wait for an answer. "Did you have parties as a child?"

She felt herself freeze up. "Sometimes."

"I suspect they weren't fun."

"No." Maybe one day she'd tell him about them but not yet. She didn't want him staying with her out of pity.

If he stayed with her at all.

"Then this was an emotional day for you," he murmured.

"And you," she said, looking back down at Megan sleeping peacefully in her crib.

"Yes. I never thought I'd love her so much."

"I feel the same."

All at once she knew she wanted more children with Matt. Her heart expanded at the thought of carrying another baby of his, this time with him playing a major part. He'd be tender toward her for sure. She could see him in her mind's eye, running his hands over her expanding waistline, leaning forward to kiss their baby through her protruding stomach.

Buoyed by the warm feelings between them, she decided to test the waters. "I love being a mother. One day I'd love to have more children like Megan."

There was a moment of silence.

Then, "How many?" he said in a clipped tone that should have forewarned her but didn't.

"Three or four. I want a big family." She kept her eyes lowered to Megan. "Would you like to have more children, Matt?"

Another moment crept by.

"Eventually," he said, a coolness to him now that was hard to miss. It filled her with dismay. This discussion was obviously not to his liking.

He turned away, tension coming off him in waves. "I've got some work to do in the study."

Her heart broke in two as he left. It was clear he had no intention of falling in love with her or extending their marriage, or having more children with her.

With a sense of desolation she showered and went to bed. Matt joined her sometime in the early hours and she fully expected him to turn his back on her and go to sleep, but he pulled her into his arms and made love to her with an edge that stabbed at the pieces of her heart.

He brought her to climax, then reached his own climax, but there was none of the usual feeling of togetherness they shared.

One thing was apparent now.

They might be together in bed.

But they weren't—and never would be—together in their hearts.

Ten

Matt got through Sunday by keeping to himself, and then Monday at work was slower as he kept trying to keep his mind on the balance sheets, only it wasn't working.

He would never have believed how much he loved his daughter, and how great it had felt to share her first words with Lana. But did she have to go and spoil it all by saying she wanted more children one day in the future?

God, he hated the thought of another man in his daughter's life. Bloody hell, but he couldn't bear to think of Megan having stepsisters and stepbrothers, and calling another man "Da-Da."

And to think of Lana with another man…

He felt as if he'd been stabbed in the gut thinking about her marrying another man, making love to someone else, carrying that other man's child. Just the thought of it had him wanting to rip any man's throat out who came near her.

Yet she'd said it so calmly, as if it were nothing out of the ordinary. He hadn't needed to know she was already thinking of being with another man before she'd even left *him*.

"Matt?"

He spun his leather chair away from the window. The million-dollar view of Sydney Harbour was worth nothing to him right now.

"I'm leaving now for my three o'clock dental appointment," Irene reminded him. "I'll see you tomorrow. If you need anything just ask Evan."

"Fine. See you tomorrow." He doubted he'd get much work done this afternoon now. All he could think about was going home and seeing Megan and Lana, who was at home on her day off.

He missed them, dammit.

Maybe he should go home early?

He sighed and straightened in his chair. No, he'd better stay here and finish up this lot of accounts. They needed reviewing by tomorrow.

Half an hour later, Matt was sitting up much straighter in his chair. "Christ!"

He didn't believe it.

He couldn't believe it.

He hadn't been looking for any anomalies, but

fifty thousand dollars was missing from one of the accounts. It was a brilliant piece of cover-up, but even more brilliant was that the money had been stolen at a time Lana wasn't working for them.

He knew who the thief was now.

Irene.

His PA.

He fell back against his chair stunned but greatly relieved. It proved to him that Lana was innocent— what he'd put her through with his accusations. She'd be relieved to know he'd found the culprit.

He knew his longtime PA was the thief just by something in the way she had fiddled the books. It had her stamp all over it. He just hadn't been looking beyond Lana before.

But what if Irene denied it? She was a personal assistant, not an accountant. She could make a fairly believable case that she couldn't possibly know how to fix the books.

Would the authorities believe her?

He dared not risk it. He had to set up a trap. An after-hours one because that's the only time Irene could have accessed the accounts without anyone getting suspicious.

But first he had to go and confess everything to Alex and Nick. They weren't going to be pleased that he'd kept the missing money from them, nor that he'd blamed Lana. They'd understand that he'd been trying to keep it quiet for their father's sake after his heart attack, but now it really was time for them to call in the police.

As for Lana, he'd sort all this out before telling her. It was the right thing to do.

After all his accusations, he owed her that much.

Lana's heart plummeted when Matt called to say he would be working late. He'd been aloof ever since Saturday night. Why had she mentioned having more children? She must have scared him off.

Sure, he was good with Megan but clearly he didn't want more children or a longer marriage to her. And clearly he wasn't about to fall in love with her. She should have kept quiet and been thankful he was a good father to Megan and a good, if temporary, husband to her.

He didn't come home until after ten that night. She'd given up and gone to bed, pretending to be asleep when he entered the bedroom and took a shower, then slid naked between the sheets, where he rolled over and went to sleep.

She wanted to say, "Hold me. Don't push me away like this," but what would be the use? She didn't want any man holding her against his will.

Somehow Lana managed to get through the next day at work without giving away her feelings. And then Matt took her home before saying he was going back to work. He kissed Megan goodbye, even gave *her* a quick kiss, but avoided looking at her and left.

Lana wanted to cry. It was obvious now what was going on. Her suggestion of more children had def-

initely driven him away—right into the arms of
another woman.

Oh God. How could she continue to live with a
man who was cheating on her? Would the next step
be that he didn't come home one night at all? How
long before it became a regular occurrence?

Like her father.

The thought panicked her, but somehow she held
herself together. At least she knew she was prepared
for the worst, and that gave her an inner strength.

He didn't make love to her that night either, not
that she expected he would try. And if he *had* tried
she certainly would have told him what she
thought of him.

After the third night of his dropping her at home
and saying he had to go back to work, Lana's heartache was overtaken by an escalating anger. So, he was
working, was he? Perhaps she'd just go down there
after Megan was in bed and check if that was true.

And if it was?

One step at a time.

At seven-thirty she asked Ruth to babysit Megan,
then hopped into her own car and drove back to the
office.

She parked in the underground car park, which
was well lit but deserted, rather than drive around to
the front entrance where the security guard would be.

With a shaky hand she punched in the code to
access the gate to the car park, her heart trembling
a minute later when she saw that Matt's car wasn't

there. She should go home right now, yet something forced her to go upstairs and check for sure that he wasn't working. She wanted no doubts about any of this.

All seemed quiet as she rode the elevator to the eighth floor. She was vaguely aware of its being eerie here, but her thoughts were on Matt and what she would find.

Or *not* find.

The door opened with a ping. And Lana's eyes widened at the scene before her. There seemed to be people everywhere, some men in suits and a couple of policemen. Alex and Nick were there and had turned to look at her, but she couldn't see—

"Matt!" she said, rushing forward with intense relief when one of the men moved and she saw Matt standing there.

He suddenly saw her and he scowled. "Lana! What are you doing here?"

She rushed up to him, putting her hands on his arm, needing to touch him. "I thought…" It didn't matter now. "Matt, what's going on? Are you okay? Is someone hurt? What happened?" She fired the questions at him, unable to stop herself from babbling.

"It's Irene. She—"

"She's been hurt? Oh my God!"

His mouth flattened in a grim line. "No, she's not hurt, Lana. She's our thief. The police are here to arrest her. She's in my office, but they'll soon be taking her down to the police station."

Lana tried to take in what he was saying. "*Irene* stole the money?"

He nodded. "I discovered another amount missing on Monday and decided to set a trap for her."

Just then Irene came out of Matt's office in handcuffs with a policeman. "You've got no proof I did anything, Matt."

Matt pointed to the potted plant on the filing cabinet. "It's all on tape, Irene. I'm not stupid, you know. I put a camera behind the plant."

She lifted her head. "I'll see you in court, *Mr. Valente*," she spat as they took her to one of the elevators.

Lana watched the exchange, stunned by Irene's changed demeanor, even as she registered one fact. Matt knew all this on Monday and hadn't told her. He'd kept it to himself.

For a few minutes she just stood there as the elevator doors closed with Irene inside.

"Lana, why—"

She rounded on him. "How *could* you, Matt?"

He frowned. "What's the matter?"

She lifted her chin. "Why didn't you tell me?"

He opened his mouth to speak, then suddenly seemed to realize they had an audience. He took her by the arm and marched her into his office, where he shut the door behind him and stood in front of it.

"Now listen to me, Lana. I was trying to protect you."

"From what?" she scoffed. "Irene?"

His mouth tightened. "Yes. You have to admit she isn't the person we knew her to be. She has a gambling problem."

That wasn't good enough.

"I would have been right there beside you helping to trap her. I don't know what she could have done to me."

"She could have lured you away on some pretext or other. She could have hurt you." Something flared in his eyes. "I didn't know what she was capable of. I couldn't take that chance."

Okay, so he had a point but...

"The thing is you didn't trust me enough to tell me. You trusted Alex and Nick but not me."

"Alex and Nick are—"

"Family?" she snapped.

"No, I was going to say they are management. I had to let my brothers know what was going on."

She understood that, too, but...

"You're missing the point, Matt. You accused me of stealing a great deal of money, yet you couldn't even ask me to help you trap the real thief? And then you let me believe that..." She trailed away.

"What?"

She swallowed past her dry throat. "That you were having an affair."

"What!"

She stiffened. "What did you expect me to think, Matt? You've been working late every evening this week. Wasn't it reasonable to think you were having an affair?"

"No. And I *was* working late. I was trying to catch Irene in the act."

Lana winced as they came back full circle. Whether it was about him not trusting her enough to tell her about Irene, or shutting her out until she thought he was having an affair, they were clearly lacking in trust.

And if they couldn't trust each other, how could their marriage survive?

He scowled. "Where's all this coming from? I promised you I wouldn't have any affairs while we were married, and I haven't."

"You said that, but—"

Someone knocked on the door. "Mr. Valente, I need to get a statement from you," one of the policemen interrupted.

"In a minute," Matt growled loudly. "Lana we need to talk. I—"

She pulled her shoulders back. "No more talk. Just leave me alone, Matt."

"No, you—"

There was another knock on the door, and frustration and anger swept over his features as he glanced back at it, then back at her. "Fine. You've got it." He spun away and stalked out of the room.

Lana stood there for a moment then left the room, too. She didn't look at anyone as she walked to the elevator, not even relaxing once the doors

closed. Her mind was too full of her emotions.
There was so much anger and hurt between her and
Matt now. So much mistrust. How long before the
raised voices started between them?

Like her parents.

She'd lie in bed and listen to their arguments and
flinch at every word until her father stormed out to
spend the night with some other woman.

She flinched now. Up until this evening she had
fooled herself into believing she could get through
the year without upsetting Megan.

But this was the moment where she knew what
she had to do. She would never let Megan go
through what she had gone through growing up.
She'd made that promise to her daughter when
she'd been born.

She would keep that promise now.

Eleven

Megan was awake and fretful when Lana got home, and Ruth was nursing her back to sleep.

"That's okay, Ruth. I'll take care of her now."

"If you're sure."

Lana nodded, desperate to get some time alone before she fell apart. She needed time to think, had to put one foot in front of the other. She'd have to find a new job and another place to live, her apartment having already been rented out. The thought of it all swamped her like a tidal wave. There was so much to do.

She wasn't sure how long it was before she looked up from rocking Megan in her arms and saw Matt in the bedroom doorway.

He'd followed her.

"Is she okay?" he asked quietly, his brown eyes dark and unreadable.

Lana rocked her. "She will be."

"Come into the living room when you've finished."

"It might be awhile."

"I'll wait."

That sounded ominous.

Fifteen minutes later, with Megan settled in her crib. Lana straightened her shoulders and walked toward the living room. As she got closer, she heard Matt's voice.

"You were the one who told me to marry her, Dad," he was saying into his cell phone, his back to her.

There was a pause.

"Yeah, like you forced Alex and Nick to marry, as well."

There was another pause.

"I'm not sure what I'll do yet."

Lana felt like her breath had been cut off. He was talking about *her*.

And what was this about Alex and Nick? Cesare had forced them to marry their wives? He'd forced Matt to marry her, too?

God, how many lives were the Valentes prepared to wreck for the sake of the family name? They'd certainly ruined hers.

She must have made a noise, because Matt spun around and saw her. "Dad, I have to go." He switched off his phone.

Lana swallowed with anguish. "Don't worry, Matt. I'll make it easy for you. Megan and I will be gone by the time you get home tomorrow."

Matt looked at his wife standing there in the doorway and something erupted inside him. He jumped to his feet. "The hell you will!"

Her chin rose in the air. "Matt, you can't stop me."

He strode toward her and put his hand on her arm, not tight but enough to bring her fully into the living room. "Right, let's talk." He slammed her with his eyes. "And I mean let's *really* talk this time."

She fixed him with a piercing gaze, then took a few steps away, forcing him to let her go. "Don't pretend, Matt. We both know you married me for Megan's sake."

He frowned. "That's right. So what's the problem?"

"But I didn't know your father had pressured you into it."

"He didn't."

She shot him a withering look. "Now who's lying? I heard you a moment ago. You reminded Cesare how he'd told you to marry me."

He waved a dismissive hand. "I was being sarcastic. He did tell me to marry you, but *I* made the decision to marry you, not him. There's a difference."

Her brow rose. "Different to Alex and Nick? How pleased you must feel to be one step ahead of them all," she said, sneering. "The youngest brother jumping in and sacrificing himself on the marriage altar would definitely make you a big man in their eyes."

What on earth…

He swore. "It wasn't like that."

"Then what was it like?"

"You already know all there is to know, Lana. I don't have an agenda."

She held his gaze and he held hers, then her shoulders suddenly drooped as all the puff seemed to leave her. "Matt, our marriage isn't working. Megan has your name now, so there's no further need for us to stay together. She's a Valente. I'll make sure she's proud of it."

Jealousy stabbed at him. "Even when you marry someone else?" he said in a harsh voice.

She looked baffled. "What do you mean?"

His muscles bunched at the thought of her with someone else. "You said you wanted more children."

"I do."

"I'm assuming you have someone in mind to father those children."

The air seemed to suddenly suspend itself.

"Of course."

Matt saw red. "The poor bastard."

Her forehead creased. "Matt, do you think—" She broke off. "It's *you* I wanted to father my children."

The blood rushed to his head. "Me?"

She met his eyes without flinching. "I wanted to have more children with you, only, you turned all cold on me and I knew I was grasping at straws to think you'd feel the same."

Matt was trying to take it all in. "You said 'wanted.' Is that feeling in the past?"

She swallowed hard. "No."

Hope began to rise inside his chest. "Then—"

"No, Matt. It can't be."

"Why not?"

She shrugged and looked away uncomfortably. "Because."

He took some steps toward her and put his hand under her chin, turning her to look at him. He wasn't going to let up. "Because?"

She lowered her eyelids, then slowly lifted them open, her feelings clear to see. "Because I love you, Matt."

A wave rolled inside Matt's chest. "You love me?" he rasped.

"Yes," she whispered. Then she stepped back, breaking away from his touch. "But it's not enough. I can't let Megan suffer in the future at our lack of trust for each other. I suffered growing up because my mother was pregnant and because my father did the right thing in marrying her, but I can't do that to Megan. My parents ended up hating each other. My father was always cheating on my mother."

He quelled a squeezing pain inside himself. "Your father married your mother because she was pregnant with you?"

She nodded. "Yes. I told you."

"No, you told me they had an abusive marriage. You didn't say why."

"Oh." Her expression clouded over, clearly with unhappy thoughts. "Well, that's why. I was always in the middle. It wasn't a pleasant feeling."

"That wouldn't happen with us."

"It happened tonight. We've already argued about Irene and about your affairs and—"

"I haven't had any affairs. Anyway, who said we would be arguing in years to come?"

"If we don't trust each other now, we certainly won't trust each other in the future."

Everything fell into place and Matt finally understood why she hadn't told him about Megan, and why she hadn't wanted to trap him. It wasn't wholly about him not being ready to be a father, as she'd stated. That had been only an excuse.

No, the problem was that her parents had left her a legacy of trust issues. Her father's adultery was the main offender, and he could only imagine what other mental scars she had. It came down to the fact that she couldn't trust *anyone* not to hurt her or her daughter—including himself.

As he looked into her pain-filled eyes he finally understood something else. It hurt like hell when you loved someone and they were in pain.

As he loved Lana.

He knew that in one blinding moment, but amazingly he somehow held himself in check. He had to tread carefully here or he could lose her.

For good.

"Did your parents love each other, Lana?"

Her expression clouded. "My mother loved my father, but it was never reciprocated."

Relief launched through his body. This was something concrete he could use. "Our situation is different."

She shook her head. "I've just told you I love you, Matt. It's not different. It's the same situation all over again."

Love swelled inside him. "It isn't, you know. You see, your father didn't love your mother…not like I love you."

"Matt, listen. I—" Her eyes widened. "Wh… what?"

"I love you, Lana."

Hope flashed in her eyes, then died. "You're only saying that. It's not possible."

"Believe me, it's very possible. It happened. It's true." He slid his arms around her waist and brought her close. "It took the threat of you leaving me to make me realize it."

She swallowed hard. "But you don't want to stay married to me, Matt."

"I don't?"

Her eyes searched his. "What about your other women? You were going to return to them after a year, remember?"

"Darling, I didn't have nearly as many affairs before I married you as you think."

Her forehead creased. "What about those nights

you stayed out late when we were first married? I didn't want to believe you were with anyone else but—"

"I went to stay at my old apartment each night for a few hours. Alone. I admit it gave me some space. I wasn't used to being married, but there were never any other women involved."

"Oh God, that's the truth, isn't it?"

"Absolutely." His hands tightened on her waist. "I married you for Megan's sake, Lana, but I want to stay married to you for *our* sake."

Moisture glittered in her eyes. "Oh Matt."

"Stay with me, Lana. Have more children with me to share our love. Be happy and make me happy, too."

"I never let myself believe in forever, Matt." She blinked rapidly. "This time I know I can."

His heart overflowed with love as he lowered his head toward her. "Yes, darling, this time you can. Trust me."

"I do."

Epilogue

Fireworks lit up the night sky over the Valente mansion for Cesare's sixtieth birthday, and family and friends oohed and aahed over the stunning display.

Isabel Valente looked at her husband of thirty-three years, her heart swelling with love and pride. He'd come to Australia from Italy with his parents when he was twelve, made his fortune and turned the Valente name into something he was proud to pass on to his sons.

And his sons were equally as proud of their father, she knew, gazing at those three sons of her heart, despite only giving birth to one of them. They were all now happily married to wonderful, caring women and starting to raise families of their own.

Alex and Olivia had adopted Scott and Renee and would adopt more children as time moved on.

Nick and Sasha had a glow about them that made her think there might be a baby on the way soon.

And Matt and Lana had adorable little Megan, who was the apple of her youngest son's eye.

"Well, Izzie," Cesare said, slipping his arm around her waist. "I'm a very happy man now. The Valente name will carry on for a long time to come."

She smiled. The Valente men could be proud, arrogant and exasperating to the women who loved them, but when it came down to it, none of the Valente women would have it any other way.

Isabel held up her glass to her husband. "Viva Valente, darling!"

And life, glorious as it was, went on.

* * * * *

Celebrate 60 years of pure
reading pleasure with Harlequin®!

Harlequin Presents® is proud to
introduce its gripping new miniseries,
THE ROYAL HOUSE OF KAREDES.
An exquisite coronation diamond,
split as a symbol of a warring
royal family's feud, is missing!
But whoever reunites the
diamond halves will rule all....

Welcome to eight brand-new titles that
unfold to reveal the stories of kings and queens,
princes and princesses torn apart by pride
and power, but finally reunited by love.

Step into the world of Karedes with
BILLIONAIRE PRINCE, PREGNANT MISTRESS
Available July 2009
from Harlequin Presents®.

ALEXANDROS KAREDES, SNOW DUSTING the shoulders of his leather jacket and glittering like jewels in his dark hair, stood at the door. Maria felt the blood drain from her head.

"Good evening, Ms. Santos."

His voice was as she remembered it. Deep. Husky. Perfect English, but with the faintest hint of a Greek accent. And cold, as cold as it had been that awful morning she would never forget, when he'd accused her of horrible things, called her terrible names....

"Aren't you going to ask me in?"

She fought for composure. Last time they'd faced each other, they'd been on his turf. Now they were on hers. She was in command here, and that meant everything.

"There's a sign on the door downstairs," she said, her tone every bit as frigid as his. "It says, 'No soliciting or vagrants.'"

His lips drew back in a wolfish grin. "Very amusing."

"What do you want, Prince Alexandros?"

A tight smile eased across his mouth and it killed her that even now, knowing he was a vicious, arrogant man, she couldn't help but notice what a handsome mouth it was. Chiseled. Generous. Beautiful, like the rest of him, which made him living proof that beauty could, indeed, be only skin deep.

"Such formality, Maria. You were hardly so proper the last time we were together."

She knew his choice of words was deliberate. She felt her face heat; she couldn't help that but she damned well didn't have to let him lure her into a verbal sparring match.

"I'll ask you once more, your highness. What do you want?"

"Ask me in and I'll tell you."

"I have no intention of asking you in. Tell me why you're here or don't. It's your choice, just as it will be my choice to shut the door in your face."

He laughed. It infuriated her but she could hardly blame him. He was tall—six two, six three—and though he stood with one shoulder leaning against the door frame, hands tucked casually into the pockets of the jacket, his pose was deceptive. He was strong, with the leanly muscled body of a well-trained athlete.

She remembered his body with painful clarity. The feel of him under her hands. The power of him moving over her. The taste of him on her tongue.

Suddenly, he straightened, his laughter gone. "I have not come this distance to stand in your doorway," he said coldly, "and I am not going to leave until I am ready to do so. I suggest you stand aside and stop behaving like a petulant child."

A petulant child? Was that what he thought? This man who had spent hours making love to her and had then accused her of—of trading her body for profit?

Except it had not been love, it had been sex. And the sooner she got rid of him, the better.

She let go of the doorknob and stepped aside. "You have five minutes."

He strolled past her, bringing cold air and the scent of the night with him. She swung toward him, arms folded. He reached past her, pushed the door closed, then folded his arms, too. She wanted to open the door again but she'd be damned if she was going to get into a who's-in-charge-here argument with him. She was in charge, and he would surely see a tussle over the ground rules as a sign of weakness.

Instead, she looked past him at the big clock above her worktable.

"Ten seconds gone," she said briskly. "You're wasting time, your highness."

"What I have to say will take longer than five minutes."

"Then you'll just have to learn to economize. More than five minutes, I'll call the police."

Instantly, his hand was wrapped around her

wrist. He tugged her toward him, his dark-chocolate eyes almost black with anger.

"You do that and I'll tell every tabloid shark I can contact about how Maria Santos tried to buy a five-hundred-thousand-dollar commission by seducing a prince." He smiled thinly. "They'll lap it up."

* * * * *

What will it take for this
billionaire prince to realize he's falling
in love with his mistress…?
Look for
BILLIONAIRE PRINCE, PREGNANT MISTRESS
by Sandra Marton.
Available July 2009
from Harlequin Presents®.

We'll be spotlighting a different series every month throughout 2009 to celebrate our 60th anniversary.

Look for Harlequin® Presents in July!

TWO CROWNS, TWO ISLANDS, ONE LEGACY
A royal family, torn apart by pride and its lust for power, reunited by purity and passion

Step into the world of Karedes beginning this July with

BILLIONAIRE PRINCE, PREGNANT MISTRESS
by
Sandra Marton

Eight volumes to collect and treasure!

THE BELLES OF TEXAS

They're as strong as the state that raised
them. The Belle sisters aren't afraid to go
after what they want, whether it's reclaiming
their ranch or their family.

Linda Warren
Caitlyn's Prize

Thanks to her deceased father's gambling
debts, Caitlyn Belle's beloved High Five Ranch
is in dire straits. Particularly because the
will stipulates that if the ranch doesn't turn
a profit in six months, it must be sold to
Judd Calhoun—the man Caitlyn jilted
fourteen years ago. And Cait knows Judd has
been waiting a long time for his revenge....

*Look for the first book
in The Belles of Texas miniseries,
on sale in July wherever books are sold.*

You're invited to join our Tell Harlequin Reader Panel!

By joining our new reader panel you will:

- Receive Harlequin® books—they are FREE and yours to keep with no obligation to purchase anything!
- Participate in fun online surveys
- Exchange opinions and ideas with women just like you
- Have a say in our new book ideas and help us publish the best in women's fiction

In addition, you will have a chance to win great prizes and receive special gifts!
See Web site for details. Some conditions apply.
Space is limited.

To join, visit us at
www.TellHarlequin.com.

REQUEST YOUR FREE BOOKS!

2 FREE NOVELS
PLUS 2
FREE GIFTS!

Passionate, Powerful, Provocative!

YES! Please send me 2 FREE Silhouette Desire® novels and my 2 FREE gifts (gifts are worth about $10). After receiving them, if I don't wish to receive any more books, I can return the shipping statement marked "cancel". If I don't cancel, I will receive 6 brand-new novels every month and be billed just $4.05 per book in the U.S. or $4.74 per book in Canada. That's a savings of almost 15% off the cover price! It's quite a bargain! Shipping and handling is just 50¢ per book.* I understand that accepting the 2 free books and gifts places me under no obligation to buy anything. I can always return a shipment and cancel at any time. Even if I never buy another book, the two free books and gifts are mine to keep forever.   225 SDN EYMS   326 SDN EYM4

Name	(PLEASE PRINT)	

Address		Apt. #

City	State/Prov.	Zip/Postal Code

Signature (if under 18, a parent or guardian must sign)

Mail to the **Silhouette Reader Service:**
IN U.S.A.: P.O. Box 1867, Buffalo, NY 14240-1867
IN CANADA: P.O. Box 609, Fort Erie, Ontario L2A 5X3

Not valid to current subscribers of Silhouette Desire books.

Want to try two free books from another line?
Call 1-800-873-8635 or visit www.morefreebooks.com.

* Terms and prices subject to change without notice. Prices do not include applicable taxes. Sales tax applicable in N.Y. Canadian residents will be charged applicable provincial taxes and GST. Offer not valid in Quebec. This offer is limited to one order per household. All orders subject to approval. Credit or debit balances in a customer's account(s) may be offset by any other outstanding balance owed by or to the customer. Please allow 4 to 6 weeks for delivery. Offer available while quantities last.

Your Privacy: Silhouette Books is committed to protecting your privacy. Our Privacy Policy is available online at www.eHarlequin.com or upon request from the Reader Service. From time to time we make our lists of customers available to reputable third parties who may have a product or service of interest to you. If you would prefer we not share your name and address, please check here. ☐

SDES09R

In 2009 Harlequin celebrates
60 years of pure reading pleasure!

We're marking this occasion by offering
16 **FREE** full books to download and read.

Visit

www.HarlequinCelebrates.com

to choose from a variety of
great romance stories
that are absolutely **FREE!**

(Total approximate retail value of $60)

We invite you to visit and share the Web site
with your friends, family
and anyone who enjoys reading.

Silhouette® Desire

COMING NEXT MONTH
Available July 14, 2009

#1951 ROYAL SEDUCER—Michelle Celmer
Man of the Month
The prince thought his bride-to-be knew their marriage was only a diplomatic arrangement. But their passion in the bedroom tells a different story....

#1952 TAMING THE TEXAS TYCOON—
Katherine Garbera
Texas Cattleman's Club: Maverick County Millionaires
Seducing his secretary wasn't part of the plan—yet now he'll never be satisfied with just one night.

#1953 INHERITED: ONE CHILD—Day Leclaire
Billionaires and Babies
Forced to marry to keep his niece, this billionaire finds the perfect solution in his very attractive nanny...until a secret she's harboring threatens to destroy everything.

#1954 THE ILLEGITIMATE KING—Olivia Gates
The Castaldini Crown
This potential heir will only take the crown on one condition—he'll take the king's daughter with it!

#1955 MAGNATE'S MAKE-BELIEVE MISTRESS—
Bronwyn Jameson
Secretly determined to expose his housekeeper's lies, he makes her his mistress to keep her close. But little does he know that he has the wrong sister!

#1956 HAVING THE BILLIONAIRE'S BABY—
Sandra Hyatt
After one hot night with his sister's enemy, he's stunned when she reveals she's carrying his baby!

SDCNMBPA0609